INTO THE
JUNGLE

Stories for Mowgli

INTO THE
JUNGLE

Stories for Mowgli

KATHERINE RUNDELL
ILLUSTRATED BY KRISTJANA S WILLIAMS

MACMILLAN CHILDREN'S BOOKS

To the lemur ball

First published 2018 by Macmillan Children's Books
an imprint of Pan Macmillan
20 New Wharf Road, London N1 9RR
Associated companies throughout the world
www.panmacmillan.com

ISBN 978-1-5098-2231-7

1 3 5 7 9 8 6 4 2

A CIP catalogue record for this book is available from the British Library.

Printed in China

Contents

Before Mother Wolf Was a Mother, She Was a Fighter

Father Wolf wedged his human child between his paws and began to lick him clean. The child, Mowgli, crouched on all fours and gnawed a buffalo bone. He was not a tidy eater, and marrow juice ran across one cheek and into his ear. Father Wolf licked it off.

'Tell me a story?' Mowgli said.

It was a very wet day in the Seoni hills. The tangle of jungle stretched away below them, its rich green leopard-spotted with red and yellow where the trees had flowered. Mother Wolf was out hunting, down towards the river, where the bandicoot rats would be hiding. Rain thrummed down outside the cave, churning the forest floor into mud, but inside it was warm and dry. It was weather for story-telling.

'But not the one about the mongoose – I'm sick of that one.'

'Don't be impertinent.' Father Wolf laid one of his teeth against the top of Mowgli's skull and applied the lightest possible pressure. Mowgli was small but tough, with muscles that could catapult him into a tree in a single jump. Even so, it hurt.

'Ow!' Mowgli rubbed his head and glared at Father Wolf. '*Ouch!*'

The wolf said nothing, only batted Mowgli's head to the side so he could run a brisk tongue along the boy's neck.

'Fine. Sorry.' Mowgli tried to look both righteously annoyed and cajoling at once. It involved a lot of eyebrow work. 'Tell me about when you were little.'

Father Wolf shook his head and went on cleaning his son, licking hard at the dirt packed behind Mowgli's left ear.

'Please!' said Mowgli. 'I'm hungry.'

'Then eat something.'

'There's no food. And anyway, I'm hungry for stories.'

'No stories about me. I've no wish to go raking through my own fur,' Father Wolf said.

'Then tell me about when Mama was young.'

'Ah!' Father Wolf's eyes shone yellow in the light. He licked the side of Mowgli's hair in pleasure and let him go. 'Yes. That I *can* do,' he said. 'Your mother is famous from the foot of the Seoni to where the trees reach the ridge on the far side of the mountain.'

Mowgli nodded. He knew that. Everyone knew that. He stretched back luxuriously and began chewing on his toenail.

'They called her Raksha, which means "the Demon"—'

This was news to Mowgli. 'Mama isn't a demon!'

'Well, perhaps less demon than spirit: something wild and untamed. It wasn't really a compliment.'

Mowgli spat out his toenail and sat up, balling his fists. 'Who dared uncompliment Mama? I'll kill them!'

Father Wolf tapped his son gently on the side of the head with his muzzle, and Mowgli fell over, back into his father's paws.

'Mama does not need you to fight anyone for her. She can take care of herself. Stop wriggling. Do you want to hear the story, or would you rather I ask Baloo to come and teach you the hunting call of the Bengal monitor lizards?'

Mowgli shook his head and pinned his lips shut with his teeth. The call of the monitor lizards is notoriously difficult; monitor lizards are not chatty, and it is a struggle to learn the language of an animal who only makes an observation every six months.

'So,' began Father Wolf. 'Raksha was born the only she-wolf in a litter of eight cubs.

'From the day she was born, she was a fighter: all claws and teeth and bite. She chewed bones and rocks and stray feathers; sometimes she chewed her brothers. There was no need, Raksha's mother would tell her, to battle to the death over a half-chewed rabbit.

"You must work on your priorities, little one," she would say.

"Not everything has to be a battle."

The cave they lived in was halfway up the mountain, with a narrow mouth but a wide chamber, warm in the winter, and dry in the rains. It smelt reassuringly of wolf-breath and dry earth, unless the smallest of the wolf cubs, Bhedi, had farted. In the cave, they grew fast, and they grew strong.

Raksha was grey, like her brothers, but unlike her brothers the tips of her ears were black. As you know, we are born with blue eyes that later turn yellow, but one of Raksha's eyes stayed the colour of the sky. It made her easy to identify, easy to remember.

The day came when the Pack Council was held. The Chief of the Pack was, back then, a vast black she-wolf by the name of Nakha – this was when Akela was nothing more than a skinny-ribbed youngster, long before he became the Lone Wolf, the leader of all wolves.

Raksha's mother licked each of the cubs until they shone in the moonlight, and then guided and nudged and carried them as they trekked to the Rock for the Looking Over.

It was a long walk for a small cub. Soon Raksha's paws began

to burn and ache, but she refused, unlike Bhedi, to ride on her mother's back, or in her mouth.

The Law of the Jungle dictates that each new litter of cubs must be brought to the Rock so that the rest of the Pack may identify them, learn their faces, memorize their smell. Then, after the Looking Over, if a grown wolf kills a cub before it is old enough to have slaughtered its first buck, the penalty for that killing must be death.

"Run, little ones," said Raksha's mother. "Show yourself to the Pack." And she rocked her head back and howled so that the wolves would hear. "Look well, O Wolves! See my cubs: remember their faces. Look well!"

A wolf cub is, as a rule, a fragile thing: fur as fluffy as a bear's stomach, and eyes as wide open as a butterfly's wings. But there are exceptions to every rule, and Raksha was an exception. Her fur was fluffy, certainly, and her eyes were wide, but she was not fragile; already she was taller than any of her brothers, and the joints in her four legs sprang faster than the rest. The cubs tore around the Council Rock, biting at one another's necks and tails in excitement, watched carefully by the adult wolves.

Bhedi ran helter-skelter across the rock. Feverish with excitement, he bit down on the nearest tail; it happened to belong to Nakha, who swiped at him with her paw, not terribly indulgently. The blow sent him flying into Raksha's nose.

"Look where you're going, Bhedi!" said Raksha; she could feel her skin growing hot and angry under her fur. She swung out at him with her claws, but he ducked and skittered away.

Nakha looked at them, unblinking, as she stalked past. "Look well, O Wolves," she called, glaring at Bhedi's scrambling behind.

"It wasn't his fault!" said a strange cub to Raksha. He was plumpish and short-tailed, with ginger patches on his chest and front paws; until that moment, he had been sheltering at his mother's side.

"Who are you? What business is it of yours?" asked Raksha. She sounded slightly ruder than she had meant to, but it was not right, she felt, for a strange cub to be butting into business between her and her brother.

"My name's Adrak," said the strange cub. "At least, it's not my real proper name – but it means 'ginger', and my real name's the same as my father's, so the other wolves kept getting confused, so . . ."

His voice tailed off at the sight of Raksha, who was doing her best to look bored and impressive at once.

"And?" she said.

"And you're Raksha. You're the one who tried to kill a squirrel before you'd grown any teeth."

"So what if I am?" said Raksha.

"So nothing. I'm just saying."

"And you're an only-cub. You don't have brothers and sisters. That's why you're soft."

Adrak looked down at the black fur on his stomach. "I'm not soft," he said.

"I dare you, then."

"Dare me to do what?" said Adrak. "You can't just say, 'I dare you.' Dares are specific!"

Raksha considered, cleaning the

dirt from under her claws. She tried to think of the bravest, most forbidden thing they could do.

"I dare you to . . . go and bite the ancient white ape's tail! At the top of the mountain!"

Adrak glared at her. "Don't make jokes about that. The ancient ape doesn't exist."

"He does exist! I know he does – Mama said so! He lives at the top of the mountain. He spends all day filing his claws to a point, and envying us down below."

"You're not supposed to talk about him."

"Why do you care, if you don't believe in him?"

"Just don't, all right? Only a stupid newborn wouldn't know we don't speak his name."

"Fine!" Raksha bared her teeth at him to hide her embarrassment. "Then . . . I dare you to steal a bite of meat from Shere Khan's kill. He definitely does exist, because I've seen him!"

Adrak swallowed. "*The* Shere Khan?"

Shere Khan was a young tiger, barely three years old, but fully

grown and fully feared. He had been born lame, but that had not held him back from eating village children, putting whole packs of wolves in danger from the angry humans. He had been known to kill a wolf cub or two.

"You'd have to do it as well," said Adrak.

"Of course!" It had never occurred to Raksha that it might be otherwise.

"But you don't know where Shere Khan hunts!" said Bhedi, popping up from behind a cleft in the rock.

Raksha rounded on her brother. "Go away, Bhedi! This is no business of yours."

"It is! You have to let me come, or I'll tell Mother."

Raksha growled. She rolled her lips back from her teeth and bared every single fang she had at Bhedi. Bhedi began, very elaborately, to clean his whiskers. His tail, though, was quivering.

Raksha turned, so her bottom was in Bhedi's face. "Come on, Adrak. Let's go."

"Where?" asked Adrak. "Which way?"

Raksha realized she did not in fact know. "He'll be at the foot of the mountain," she said. "That's where all the buffalo are."

"But the mountain's got a really big foot," said Adrak. "Where *exactly*?"

"I know!" said Bhedi. "I heard Mother and Father talking about it."

"Where?"

"I'm not telling you," said Bhedi, "or you'll run off without me." He strutted past Raksha and looked back over his shoulder. "I'll be the leader and show you the way."

"No you won't!" Raksha pounced. She launched herself at Bhedi's throat, far harder than she ever had before. Bhedi squeaked with shock and wriggled under her. "Tell me!"

"No!"

"Tell me, or I'll pull out your whiskers!"

"You wouldn't!" It is the greatest possible insult to pull out a Wolf's whiskers.

"Wouldn't I?" Raksha took one of Bhedi's whiskers in her teeth, and gave a short, sharp tug.

"Ow! Raksha!"

"I'll do it again!"

"No, don't – ow, no! All right! He hunts in the plains where the snake stream meets the elephant pool. And I'll tell Mother what you did to me. So there."

"Good," said Raksha. She dropped her brother and strode off away from the rock, down the dry earth towards the green below them. A hot surge of guilt was beating in her blood, but she set back her ears and refused to let Adrak see it.

Behind them they heard the call: "Look well, O Wolves!" But nobody saw them go.

Adrak stumbled after her, breathing heavily through his snout.

A minute passed, and then a pure-grey shadow slipped away from the rock and followed.

The walk down to the open plains took longer than Raksha had expected. She tried to run, at first, all four paws kicking up dust into Adrak's face behind her, but soon she began to pant and wheeze, and even the satisfaction of covering her new friend in dust couldn't spur her on.

She stopped, hunkered down close to the ground, and panted.

"Are we nearly there?" gasped Adrak.

"Less than nearly, I think," said Raksha, "but more than not at all."

They were still struggling to catch their breath when they felt, rather than heard, a rumble. It vibrated in the earth under their paws and in Raksha's fur.

"Is that him?" whispered Adrak.

Raksha nodded. She tried to look more confident than she felt. "Come on! We'll find Shere Khan, creep up behind him, take a bite out of his deer or whatever it is he's caught, and then run to where the trees are so thick he can't follow."

"Right," said Adrak, nodding slowly. "The thing is . . ."

"What?"

"That sounds like a much worse plan now that we're down here than it did when we were up there."

Privately, Raksha had been thinking exactly the same thing, but hearing Adrak's doubts somehow made her feel braver.

"Nonsense!" she said, sounding very much like her Grandmother Wolf; and then she turned and ran on, following the sound of the roar, through buffalo-high grasses and away from the protection of the jungle. The little grey shadow ran after her.

The sound led them through the fields, where they caught occasional whiffs of man-smell. Adrak wrinkled his nose.

"I like it," said Raksha defiantly. "It smells delicious."

Soon they came to a watering hole, surrounded on all sides by sun-bleached grass, with a few bare trees growing nearby, and, further to the west, the fringe of the jungle, growing thick with vines and the vast deep-green leaves the wolves called Elephant Ears.

Underneath one of the bare brown trees, lying with one paw reaching out to the watering hole, was a tiger. Raksha froze. Adrak bumped into her, and then tried to freeze too. The small grey shadow, making its way through the grasses, snuffling in the sun, did not freeze.

The tiger was not hunting. It was waiting under the tree; its head turned away from

Raksha and Adrak, towards the village.

A tiger has a very specific smell to a wolf. It smells of metal and heat and spit. It smells of *take-care* and *stay-away*.

"How can we eat his kill," whispered Adrak wetly in Raksha's ear, "if he hasn't killed anything?"

"Shh!" said Raksha. "We'll have to do something else."

"Do what?"

"I don't know – maybe we bite *his* tail?"

"*You* can," said Adrak, "if you want to. I signed on for eating deer, not tiger."

"Shh! Not so loud!" said Raksha.

The tiger turned. Its eyes were bright as gold, and as hard, but the fur around its muzzle was white with age.

"It's not Shere Khan," Raksha whispered. "It's too old."

The tiger's gaze swept the open grass. Raksha felt her stomach drop towards her tail. But the tiger wasn't looking at her. It was looking to the west of her, where the long grass was moving, suddenly swishing from side to side.

Another tiger came padding towards the watering hole. In

its jaws was something Raksha and Adrak couldn't make out: a smudge of grey against the orange of the sun and of the grass and of the tiger's stripes.

The tiger limped on its front paw.

"Shere Khan," whispered Raksha. "The lame hunter."

"Shh!" said Adrak.

"What is this?" roared the older tiger. "Worm-eaten, thin-tailed disgrace to my name!"

"Father, I—" said the second tiger.

"I told you to bring me a buffalo! Or a deer – something large to calm the fury in my gut. And now, you bring me this? What is it? A rabbit? A squirrel? A fur cloak, as the humans wear? Have you brought me a coat to eat, idiot boy? I have told you before and I tell you again, you are barely half a son to me."

"A wolf cub," said Shere Khan. And he spat the shivering grey bundle at the feet of his father.

Every single hair on Raksha's back rose. The bundle gave a squeak and then, as Shere Khan gave it a great kick with his non-lame foot to send it spinning over the dry earth, fell silent.

"Bhedi," she whispered.

Adrak's eyes grew wide. Every inch of Raksha began to shake; her tail swished backwards and forwards, try as she might to still it. It rustled through the grass in which they crouched.

"Raksha!" whispered Adrak, and jerked his head at her tail. "Stop it! They'll see!"

Raksha caught her tail in her mouth and bit down hard on it. "We have to do something," she said, through her mouthful of fur. "We have to snatch him back."

"We can't!" hissed Adrak. "Shere Khan will kill us all."

"*Can't* doesn't matter." Raksha spat out her tail and rolled her lips up from her teeth. "He's my brother," she said. "*You* can do whatever you want, but I haven't got a choice. You can wait here."

She swallowed, tasting the terror in her mouth. She breathed in and crouched, sinking backwards into the earth, preparing her hind legs to spring.

Adrak leaped forward and gripped her by the scruff

of the neck, holding on tight. "Shh! You can't go leaping in there like you're going to fight to the death; you'll get us both killed. You need a plan."

"Let go of me!"

"Shh!" Adrak let go of Raksha.

She lay flat, as close to the ground as she could. Her brain spun and skittered over possible plans; every idea she had seemed more foolish and unlikely than the last.

The roar of the two tigers was growing louder.

"Food is not plentiful, Father," bellowed Shere Khan. "You speak as if it were easy! The buffalo around here are not trusting; they scatter at the merest breath of wind!"

"It *would* be easy, if you were not as lame in your brain as you are in your foot."

Bhedi lay in front of the tigers, wet with tiger spit and quaking, with his paws over his nose, too terrified to raise his head.

"Listen," whispered Raksha. "Listen: this is what we'll do." She bent down, pushed her snout into Adrak's ear, and whispered . . .

"That's a terrible plan!" he hissed. "We don't have time!"

"Do you have a better suggestion?"

"No! Of course I don't! But your plan will get all three of us killed!"

"And if we wait, Bhedi will be killed, and if he's going to die, then I might as well die too, because Mother will tear me apart with her own teeth if I return without him." Raksha wasn't sure if she was exaggerating.

Adrak let out a guttural growl of anxiety.

"You can still run home if you want to," said Raksha. "They might be fighting too loudly to hear you."

"You'd say I was soft."

"For leaving?" Raksha stared at him. "I'm not actually insane, you know! You wouldn't be soft – you'd be sensible."

Adrak hesitated. Then he shook his head. "No. I'll do what you say."

Raksha did not smile, but her thin body vibrated with something deep and gut-born. One word for it – a small, insufficient word – was "gratitude".

"On my signal?" she said.

Adrak nodded. He tried to look longer in the leg and broader in the back than he was.

"Wait here," said Raksha. "Keep your tail low."

She set off through the grass, looping around the far side of the lake, edging towards the spot where the jungle began to encroach on the fields. Adrak watched as she disappeared into the green fringe.

A horrible thought struck him. What if she wasn't coming back? What if she was running home and leaving him here, so that there would be no witnesses to what had happened?

The tigers had stopped roaring. The old tiger was spinning Bhedi in the dirt, attempting to make him uncurl his paws so he could rake a claw down the lining of his stomach.

"It squirms like a worm! You have brought me a worm for my meal!"

"Bite its head off!"

"Like a jackal? You are a grotesque misuse of tiger blood, child."

"Just do it! I'm hungry!"

"And that is no fault of mine, boy."

Suddenly, a hundred wolf-paces from the fringe, where

the grass grew high as a human Man, there was movement, a rustle and a huffing. But it was not a small rustle, made by the body of a half-year wolf cub; it was a true disturbance, of the kind made by buffalo and buck. Adrak held his breath. The tigers looked up.

"There!" roared the old tiger. "See, there – or are you blind as well as lame? See? Something in the grass! Go!"

Shere Khan let out a roar that shook the barren tree above him. He rocked back on his haunches, then leaped forward with the force of a thunderstorm. But he landed on his bad paw and rolled, roaring again, now with pain, in the dust.

"Idiot boy!" His father rose creakily to his feet. "I shall show you how a true tiger hunts."

He sprang forward and ran through the grass, a little arthritically, but still far faster than Adrak liked.

An extraordinary noise came from the grass near the jungle. A wolf cannot imitate a buffalo, but it was the closest thing possible: something between a growl and a bellow, a peculiar sound that rang through the open plain.

It was the signal. Adrak shot forward out of the grass, his paws churning up dust, and grabbed Bhedi by the neck. "Run!" he hissed. "Run to where the vines grow thickest."

It took Bhedi a moment to understand what was happening; then he jumped up and set off, weaving slightly, running as fast as his short legs would propel him. Adrak ran behind him, ready to drag him in his teeth if need be.

The green vines of the jungle were close now. Bhedi paused to catch his breath. "Where's . . . Raksha? Is . . . she—?" he panted.

"No time to talk! Run!" Adrak clouted Bhedi on the side of the head, exactly as his sister had done earlier that day. "Run!"

They did not dare turn to watch until they were right at the edge of the green shadows of the jungle; they ducked behind a tree and stared. The tigers were running – their progress slowed by the fact that the father was taking time to roar insults at his son – but they were close, now. Adrak bent and laid his chin on the floor, feeling the vibrations of the tigers' running feet.

The thing they were chasing was heading straight towards Adrak and Bhedi, straight towards the dark cover of the jungle.

"What is it?" hissed Bhedi. "A buck? A warthog?"

"It's Raksha!"

"No it's not! It's huge!"

But at that moment Raksha came into sight. She was running flat out, all four legs thumping against the ground, her tail straight out behind her. Her eyes were wild with fear. Grimly she clutched two Elephant Ear leaves in her teeth, which stuck out to either side of her, tripling the size of her shadow and fanning the grass out in a wave before her.

"Run!" called Adrak. "Run, Raksha! They're too close!"

She gave a yelp, dropped the leaves, and disappeared nose first into a tangle of vines.

"Come on!" roared Adrak. "Follow her!"

The tigers crashed after them. Raksha led the way down the inside of a hollow fallen tree, through a densely packed thorn bush, blood pearling out from their scratches. Adrak pushed Bhedi ahead of him and felt a thorn scrape down the corner of his left eye. He let out a yelp, and the siblings turned to him, half concerned, half furious.

"Don't!" said Bhedi. "He'll hear."

Adrak screwed his eyes tight and waited in the dark of the thorn bush, swallowing the angry whine that rose to his jaws. They crouched in the bush, quivering, trying not to move.

They could hear the grunt and sniff of a tiger's snout as Shere Khan moved to and fro across the forest.

"I can smell them. They're somewhere in there. Allow me a few minutes, Father, and I will drive them out, straight into your jaws."

"Leave them!" grunted the older tiger. "I have no stomach for wolf cubs."

"But, Father, three would make a meal fit for a tiger—"

"I said I have no stomach for it, and I have no stomach for your presence either." He shook his head. "Outsmarted by a wolf cub. I will go and lie in the sun." He paused, raking his son with his gaze. "If you find me dead, it will be safe to assume that I have died of shame."

Shere Khan watched his father stalk out of the jungle and back into the open sun. The deep orange fur on his shoulders shivered. He turned away from the thicket of thorns and planted himself on the ground.

Very, very slowly, Raksha started to inch through the thicket.

"Can you open your eyes?" she whispered to Adrak.

"It hurts," he breathed. "It leaks."

"Keep them closed. Take my tail in your mouth."

He followed, his eyes closed. Bhedi guided him, his snout to Adrak's rear. It didn't, in fact, help very much, and Bhedi's nose was very wet and cold and kept nudging him in the bottom, but Adrak said nothing.

They crept, low to the ground, under cover of the thorns, towards the foot of the mountain. Here the rocks led a path upward, and there would be half-formed caves where a small wolf could hide and a tiger could not follow. They started up the side of the mountain. Raksha's breath began to calm. She sped up, scattering pebbles with her front paws.

Shere Khan heard them. He turned, not as if about to spring up the mountain, but slowly, as a thundercloud turns towards the sun.

His eyes met Raksha's. He opened his jaws and gave a roar

so loud, the vibrations ran up the pads of Raksha's paws into her stomach and lungs. "You! Wolf cub! You are not yet old enough to understand how great a mistake you have made."

Raksha said nothing. Adrak opened his unscratched eye and stared down at the angry orange blur crouched below their rocky outcrop.

The tiger roared again. Raksha flattened her ears against her head.

"You do not disrespect Shere Khan without living to regret it!" said the tiger.

"Your father does," said Raksha. "We heard."

Tigers cannot blush as humans can, but they can turn hot behind the eyes. Their whiskers shake, and their tails swish in unstoppable twitches across the floor. Shere Khan's whiskers shook now, and his eyes burned up at Raksha. "There will be a reckoning, wolf-child!" he said.

Raksha looked down at the tiger from the outcrop of rock. She said nothing, only let the hackles rise along her back, the bite and hunger and valour radiate from her half-year cub's eyes.

Shere Khan looked away first.

"Come, Bhedi," she said. "Come, Adrak. We should run. He's not an animal to be trusted."'

❧

Father Wolf paused and smiled down at his son. Mowgli was sitting bolt upright, every muscle tense. He wrapped his fists around Father Wolf's yellow-flecked front paw.

'And then? Then what happened?'

'That's the end of the story.'

'But what happened to Adrak? What happened to Bhedi?'

'Bhedi grew up to be as tall as Raksha and almost as strong, though never terribly wise. But he is loved. He started a pack to the east of the Seoni hills. You may meet him one day.'

'And Adrak? Will I meet him?'

Father Wolf scratched at the scar under his left eye with his hind leg. 'Oh, yes. Adrak grew up tall enough and with a fair set of teeth, it's said. But he would still be unwilling to take on Raksha in a fight.'

Bagheera's Cage

Mowgli had just finished trimming his little toenail with his teeth when Brother Wolf came bounding up to the cave.

'Mowgli!' he called. 'There you are! Mother wants you. She says it's important.'

Mowgli's stomach sank. Two days before, he had been racing a leopard cub called Billi through the jungle, Billi haring along the forest floor and Mowgli up in the trees, when he had kicked an eagle-owl's nest to the ground.

Billi had stared at the nest with wide eyes. 'Would it be wrong to eat just one egg?' she'd asked.

'Yes!' Mowgli nipped her in the neck with his front teeth and glared at her full in the face until she backed away. 'I'd get the blame!'

Then he had gathered up the eggs, placed them back in the nest and returned it to its place in the tree. None of the eggs were broken, but one of them had cracked, a hairline lightning bolt pointing accusingly up at him. He had twisted the egg around so that the crack wouldn't show, his heart thumping. Some of the nest's twigs stuck out at peculiar angles, and his attempt to neaten them only made it worse. He had hoped very much that the owl wouldn't notice; clearly, though, she had.

Mother Wolf rarely punished her cubs, but when she did, she used every single one of her teeth.

Mowgli did not hesitate. He sprinted to the nearest tree, swung himself up into the leafy safety of the canopy, and took off running along the thickest branch.

'Mowgli!' howled Father Wolf.

'No, wait! It's important!' called Brother Wolf. 'She says—'

But Mowgli was already out of earshot. He did not hear Brother Wolf's final words, did not hear them echo after him: 'She says you're in danger!' He did not see the fear in Brother Wolf's eyes.

Mowgli kept scrambling across the treetops, skinning his elbow on a rough cedar, barely stopping to wipe off the blood, until he reached the mango grove. Then he paused, listening for wolves. He hung upside down from his knees and surveyed the world below.

The jungle unfurled in every direction, green and brown intricately entwined. He could see vines and flowers curling around fallen tree trunks, and the disappearing tail of an alarmed mongoose. The air smelt of sun on wet earth. If he closed his eyes and blocked his ears and concentrated very hard, he could also smell the feet of the caterpillars – a tangy, acidic smell – and the presence, somewhere nearby, of lizards. It smelt of things growing and decaying and rising up again. It smelt of home.

He swung himself upright, jumped on to a new branch, and

reached for a mango. With a sharp crack, the branch snapped suddenly under his feet. He grabbed wildly for a nearby vine, missed, and landed on the moving back of an elephant.

It was a shock, to say the least. An elephant's back is stuck full of short bristles, and the skin scraped against Mowgli's legs as he slid down, as fast and gently as he could, to the ground.

Luckily it was an elephant he knew a little. Rapi was gentle-eyed and soft-eared, and would be relatively unlikely to crush him out of annoyance.

Mowgli scrambled to his feet. 'I do apologize!' he said politely, for elephants are the true Kings and Queens of the Jungle, and it does not do to forget it. 'Pray forgive me!'

Rapi laughed down at him. 'It serves me right for going anywhere near a man-cub's cave. Like with a coconut tree, you're sure to get hit eventually. Come, sit down here. Tell me about the Wolf Pack. How many are you now?'

Mowgli ran through the names of the newest litter. He could see Rapi memorizing them: it is an elephant's job to know all the life of the jungle. He slowed down his recitation, to give her time.

'And Bagheera the panther?' said Rapi. 'When last I saw him, he said he was teaching you to hunt – how is he?'

'What?' Mowgli turned wide eyes on the elephant. 'You know Bagheera?'

'I knew Bagheera years before you were born,' said Rapi. She smiled sternly at him and shook her head. 'You are not the oldest, nor the wisest, creature in the jungle.'

Mowgli laid one excited, incautious hand on the elephant's trunk. 'What was he like, back then? When he was a cub?'

'Like? What was Bagheera like? That is a more complicated question than you know.'

'Tell me!' said Mowgli. And then, as the elephant gave him a look as large as her own body, he added, 'If you would be so kind.'

The elephant's small eyes looked past Mowgli, out towards the jungle path and, far, far beyond, towards the city.

'Bagheera was born in a city, in a palace, in a cage,' she began. 'He wore a red silken collar. He chewed at it until they replaced it, this time with one of thick cow hide, which rubbed away the fur around his neck.

The floor of the cage was straw, and the bars were iron. The lock, though, was solid silver. All the Maharana's cages had silver locks, and he carried silver keys at his waist, in case he wanted to open them.

He did not – very wisely – want to open Bagheera's cage.

The City Palace in Udaipur rose in great carved columns to the sky. Behind the high white walls were gardens, pools of water dotted with lotus flowers, and a series of smaller buildings; three of these housed the menagerie. The smallest held just two cages; one of them was Bagheera's.

The cage was big enough for three paces to the wall and three paces back. At dawn, before the day grew hot, two men came to feed Bagheera with chunks of meat thrown into an iron pan; they would stare at him, but they never dared reach into the enclosure. Bagheera would bare his teeth at them and growl deep in his throat; even at two years old, he was wide-shouldered and fast-clawed. There was a look in his eyes that said he would

eat any hand that came near him.

The only other cage in the room was set to the left of Bagheera's, too far to touch with his paw: it belonged to his little sister, Gilhari. The name meant "squirrel", chosen by their mother because she had been so quick-footed and nervy as a cub.

Her collar was gold silk; unlike Bagheera, she had not chewed hers up into pulp, for she feared the leather replacement. She was as slight as Bagheera was broad, and her black was less inky than his; in sunlight you could see the markings of the leopard shining through her fur.

Sunlight, though, was a thing they barely knew. The only sun either of them ever saw came filtered through the single high window above their cages. The window did not open. They had never felt the earth under their paws, never seen a tree grow from the ground. They knew only iron, and brick, and the rattle of keys.

Sometimes, while she slept, the men put their hands through the bars and stroked Gilhari's back. Bagheera would growl, as deep in his throat as he knew how, but it didn't stop them. Bagheera took care to sleep in the exact centre of his cage so they could never touch him. In truth, they wouldn't have dared touch him even in his sleep; they did not trust him. They were right not to.

One day, though, a sudden change came to the menagerie. A gang of high-born boys, playing outside in the courtyard, sent a ball flying through the high window in the menagerie wall. Shards of glass clattered down into Gilhari's cage. Gilhari roared, skittering to the side of the cage, crushing her body against the bars in a bid to escape the glass.

The menagerie keepers panicked.

"If she cuts herself, the Maharana will have us both fired! He doesn't want his panthers all cut up."

"What do we do, then?"

"I don't know! I'm not going in there to sweep up the glass! She'll chew my face off!"

Bagheera, on the other hand, did not panic. He sat, breathing in and out in great gulps.

The smell that came through the broken window was unlike anything Bagheera had encountered. He did not hear the keepers

roaring, did not hear Gilhari snort and huff as she batted at the broken glass in her cage. He could do nothing but sniff the air, half drunk on the scent of it.

The smell was full of wild detail. It smelt of passion-fruit vines pushing up from under the dirt, of the passing of elephants with maharanis on their backs, of human sweat and monkey sweat and sun. It was the smell of outside; the smell of living things.

An animal roar made Bagheera whip round. The men were trying to slide a stick with a hook at the end on to Gilhari's collar through the door. They hauled her out of her cage on the end of the stick.

"Back!" she roared at them. "Get away from me!"

Suddenly Bagheera felt something heavy and metal hook round the edge of his own collar, and he too was hauled against the bars of his cage, half choking and spitting with rage. The door of his world flew open, Gilhari was thrust in, and the silver lock clanged shut. The hook was unhitched from Bagheera's throat. The two were together.

The menagerie men began sweeping the glass from Gilhari's cage. They spoke in their own language, their faces wrinkled in a way Bagheera had learned meant either annoyance or that they were about to expel a loud and unpleasant gust of wind.

Bagheera and Gilhari stayed at opposite sides of the cage, staring at each other. Never since the day after Gilhari was born had they been close enough to touch. Gilhari was quivering.

The men brushed down the rest of the glass from the high window and went out. The door slammed behind them. There were just the two panthers, alone.

Gilhari launched herself at Bagheera. She tugged at the scruff of his neck and licked his muzzle and the insides of his ears, licked his eyes and paws and tail, chewed lovingly on the tip of his nose.

"My brother!" she said. "After so long!"

"Are you hurt? Did the glass cut you?"

"Not at all. I thought it was the thing Mama used to call rain, at first," she said, "but then I remembered: Mama said rain changes shape when you touch it, and the glass didn't."

"You're lying! You *are* hurt. There, your paw – it's bleeding!"

Gilhari dismissed it with a butt of her head against her brother's chest. "Why are you wasting time over that? Play with me!" And she launched herself at Bagheera, trying to bite his tail.

Bagheera was a full year older than Gilhari, but he was not too old to play. He crouched and leaped clean over Gilhari's back, almost grazing his head against the roof of the cage, landing behind her. He seized the tip of her tail in his jaws.

"Ow! Too hard! You don't know how strong you are!"

"Sorry!" He had not been within touching distance of another animal for so long.

They invented a game in which one leaped over the other's back, somersaulted, and came up nose to nose, teeth bared, trying not to laugh.

That night, for the first time, the two panthers felt the coolness of the evening breeze on their fur, on the skin of their muzzles, on their tongues. With no glass in the window, the smells of the palace gardens crowded in as the night fell; they could smell dew and the scents of unidentifiable animals coming out to hunt.

"Is that jackal? Or wild dog?" said Gilhari. "Mama said wild dogs smell of spit."

The smell was alive. It wove itself into Bagheera's blood; it poked and prodded at his skin; it blew a new unruly courage into his heart.

"I don't know," he said. "Let's go and see!"

"Bagheera, don't." Gilhari's voice was soft and suddenly sad. "Please don't tease."

"You just said I don't know my own strength. What if it's true?"

"Bagheera! Don't do anything stupid! They'll punish you. I couldn't bear to be here alone!"

But Bagheera wasn't listening. He approached the lock. The light of the moon shone through the window and made the silver shimmer as if alive.

Bagheera put out a paw and tapped it. Gilhari rocked back on her haunches, her back bristling. Then Bagheera drew back his paw and swiped at the lock with one great blow. It cracked. A fault line ran down the left-hand side where it had been joined to the iron bars. Gilhari gasped. Bagheera nudged the lock with his nose. It clattered to the floor.

The noise was louder than they had expected, and they froze, waiting for the guards to come running. But the only sound was the call of the crickets outside, and the burbling, bubble-blowing sound of the frogs' love call.

Gilhari pushed open the cage door with her nose. She began to run in wild circles around the outside of their two cages, growling and quaking and huffing with excitement.

"Come," said Bagheera. "Let's go and see what that smell is."

"We can't!" said Gilhari. "The window's too high."

"It isn't," said Bagheera. "We're panthers. Panthers can jump as high as the tallest trees. Mama told me."

"When?"

"Before you were born. Before she died."

"Liar!"

"Am not!"

Bagheera was in fact lying. But the window did not look so terribly high. Not to an animal with spring and fire in his muscles.

"You go first," he said.

"Why?"

"Because I'm bigger! If you can do it, I can, and I don't want you to be left here if it turns out you can't."

"I'd be fine, thank you very much."

Bagheera said nothing.

Gilhari pulled back her gums to expose her teeth; it made her look angry, but in fact Bagheera knew it was more complicated than that: it was fear and excitement and hope and mistrust rolled into one grimace.

"Go on!"

"But what if it's not good out there?" she asked. "We get fed in here; we get water."

"But you say every day you want to leave!"

"I know! I know. But what if there's nothing out there for us?"

"We'll stick together! I'll make sure you have food! I'm your brother. I won't let anything hurt you."

"Really?"

"Yes! I swear it! Now jump, before they come back!"

Gilhari faced the window. She rocked back on her haunches, tensed every muscle, and jumped. She went sailing, head first, into the wall.

She landed, glared at him, daring him to laugh, shook the dizziness out of her skull, and jumped again. This time she sprang up and landed with her head and forepaws sticking out of the window. There was a moment of scrabbling and grunting, and then she disappeared into the night.

Bagheera crouched, drew breath, and launched himself at the window. He felt the remaining shards of glass at the base of the windowsill catch against his fur, and then, suddenly, his front paws thumped against dry earth, and he somersaulted over and over in the grass of the Maharana's gardens. He let out a short, quickly stifled roar.

The menagerie house was in the centre of a great sweep of green lawn; to each side of it were flower beds, thick with roses and marigolds and scented with jasmine. Beyond that, there was a wide stone path. At one end of it was a great iron gate, like a far vaster version of Bagheera's cage bars; at the other end of it, the main building of the palace shone white in the moonlight. There was a vast pool of water in front of the palace, from the middle of which a stream of water seemed to be raining upward. Its rush and hiss was the only sound in the stillness of the night air.

Bagheera's instinct rose up in him like a roar, and he felt an almost overwhelming urge to tear across the grass and leap into the raining pool. But he restrained himself and turned to Gilhari. Gilhari was bleeding from where her stomach had landed on the windowsill, but she did not seem to have noticed. Her eyes were brighter than Bagheera had ever seen them, and she was performing a panther's dance, something like a one-panther two-step, on the smooth lawn.

"Quick! We need to get out of here!" said Bagheera. A clump of rhododendron bushes grew close by, and Bagheera led his sister to crouch in them. "We need to decide: where now?"

"To the jungle, of course! Where Mama came

from!" Gilhari paused. "Which way is that?"

Bagheera sniffed. The air came in ten dozen layers: human smells, of metal and woven cloth, then horse dung and roadside bonfires, and then dogs and rats, all the way down to ants and bees. Ants smell cleaner than bees. And then there was one more smell: that of a thousand green cells growing, pushing out buds and transforming earth and water into life, anchoring the sun into the ground.

"Can you smell that? Like the scent of hordes of things growing together, all at once?"

"Yes! I smell it! How could I not? It's . . . almost solid. It's the kind of smell you could bite chunks out of." Gilhari snapped her jaws at the air, giddy, shaking with the joy of it.

"I think that's the smell of the jungle."

"How can you be sure?"

"What else could it be?"

"Then we'll need to go that way!" And Gilhari swung her head in the direction of the smell, towards the

great mountain in the west. "Out that way. Through those iron palace gates!"

They stared at each other, suddenly shocked by their own mad daring.

"I think," said Gilhari, "we just charge. We'll run at the iron gate, and the guards will get out of our way. Come on!" Her black tail was whirring in circles.

Bagheera looked at her as she crouched, rhododendron leaves covering her back. She was a peculiar mix of timidity and recklessness, of wild and tame – but most of all, she was his. His blood, his charge, his sister.

"No! Mama said I had to look after you. And looking after you means not letting you do anything that will get you shot."

"We have to do something quickly! They'll notice we're gone!"

"We're not just charging. We need to hide and think."

"Then let's hide over there!" She jerked her head towards the pool of water. "Mama said rain comes from the sky to the ground, but this is the opposite – I want to see it!"

Before Bagheera could stop her, Gilhari had leaped forward.

He grabbed the tip of her tail in his mouth, and she spun round with an indignant squeak.

"Keep low!" he hissed.

They crept as silently as they could from rhododendron bush to rhododendron bush, keeping their stomachs low against the grass, edging towards the great marble pool. Then they dashed across the path towards it, slipped up over the edge and, as silently as they could, into the water. They ducked their heads down low, below the parapet.

Gilhari could not suppress a snort of shock and joy as the water closed over her body. It came up to Bagheera's shoulders and lapped cool and fresh against his chin. It felt like being encased in a promise.

They edged further into the fountain, closer to the upward rain. Gilhari thrust her face into the stream of water.

"Look!" said Gilhari. "The water doesn't come from the earth at all!"

It came from a pipe, set in the marble floor of the pool. Bagheera watched as the water sprang upward from it with a ferocious gush.

"It sounds like the roar the sky makes – Mother used to call it thunder," he said.

Gilhari gave a sudden growl of excitement. "That noise! That's how we'll get them to move away from the gate!"

"How?" asked Bagheera.

"That upward water! It's loud, isn't it? Like thunder?"

"I just said that."

"And so, if it stopped, they would come and look, wouldn't they?"

"I imagine so."

"And panthers can outrun humans, can't we?"

"Yes." Bagheera sounded far more sure than he actually was, but right that second, his muscles were so full of compressed energy, he felt he could outrun time itself.

"Then this is my plan," said Gilhari. She bent her head to his.

Spray speckled Bagheera's face as he listened. When she

finished, the brother and sister looked at each other, then back at the guards. Bagheera nodded. He felt a spark of fear and excitement flash between them.

They edged closer to the pipe, right up to the heart of the upward stream, the water cascading down on their shoulders and noses and eyes. Bagheera shook himself as Gilhari pressed her black silk forepaws over the top of the pipe.

"Ow!" she cried. "The water's strong!"

Bagheera added his paws on top of hers. The water thundering upward slowed, first to a rivulet, and then, as they pressed down harder, to the merest trickle.

Down at the iron gate, the two guards turned to each other.

"Does something feel different to you?" said one.

The second guard sniffed the air. "I don't know . . . Yes! It's quieter."

"The fountain!" said the first guard. "Look! It's stopped."

"Must be something blocking the spout."

"Better go see."

Inside the fountain, soaked, water trickling inside their ears, the two panthers waited, their paws shuddering with effort, their muscles aching with fear.

Then Bagheera stiffened. He could hear the crunch of footsteps approaching: two sets of footsteps.

What happened next happened very fast. The two guards peered over the edge of the fountain. They blinked. Two sets of golden eyes blinked back. And then there was an eruption of pent-up water and of black fur as two silken creatures leaped clean over the guards' heads and hurtled, flying black shadows, down the path towards the gate. The guards, soaked and bewildered, turned to fumble for their guns, but found them drenched, the barrels full of water. They dropped them and began to run.

Gilhari reached the gate first and slipped through, her narrow shoulders passing easily between the bars. Bagheera launched himself after her. A sudden agonizing pain caught at his ribs: he was stuck.

One of the guards was almost upon them, his finger pointing in the moonlight. "Stop them!" he roared.

Gilhari turned at the noise. She hurtled back towards the gate and reached Bagheera just as the man seized hold of her brother's tail.

With one great swipe of her paw, she raked her claws down the back of the man's hand. The man screamed and let go.

"Nobody touches my brother!" she snarled. "No human will ever touch my brother again!"

Gilhari seized Bagheera's collar in her teeth and pulled. His ribs shrieked in agony, and then suddenly he was through, bruised to the bone, but free and on the road in front of the palace. He could feel, rather than hear, running footsteps.

"More men are coming," he said. "Run!"

They charged, neck and neck, down the wide road, down a smaller dirt road, past an astonished old man leaning against a cart and chewing paan in the moonlight, who spat his mouthful out in shock as they hurtled by, and then, suddenly, they were in sight of long grass. They veered into it.

"This way!" called Gilhari. "I can smell it!"

They ran through grass, on and on, and as they ran, Bagheera felt the earth grow softer under his paws; it had not

been packed down by human feet and horses' hoofs. Loose earth spurted up behind him in an arc.

The edge of the jungle lay ahead of them; humankind had beaten it back, but here it began to encroach on the fields. Here they could see ferns springing up among crops, Elephant Ears waving among corn – and then suddenly they were in among the trees. The trees grew thicker and thicker, the earth damper, the smell more and more intense until it swept over them, and they collapsed, rolling on their backs, panting and laughing, drunk on the smell of the wild.

Gilhari began to chew at Bagheera's throat.

"What are you doing?"

"Taking off that collar."

"Ow! That's not the collar – ow! – that's my skin!"

It took a long time, but at last the collar lay discarded in the dirt. Bagheera began to dig. He had never dug in the earth before; it felt extraordinary, to scoop the soil out behind the pads of his paws and feel his strength force the mud to give way. He swept the collar into the hole with a flick of his tail. With one bite he tore off Gilhari's gold silk, and it followed. Together, they refilled the hole. Then they lay upon it and stared at each other, hardly daring to believe what they had done.

The sun was just rising over the trees stretched high above their heads, flowering in white and red and purple. Bees buzzed around a honeycomb; a young monkey ran down a tree head first, spotted the two panthers, squeaked, and abruptly disappeared into the leaves.

"So this is the world that Mama told us about," said Gilhari.

Bagheera dipped his nose to the ground. His whiskers twitched. He could almost hear it growing, almost feel the vibrations in the tips of his fur. "This is the jungle." He raised his head and looked up at the sun.

"Let's hunt!"

The next four moon-cycles passed in a blur of joy and eating. They went far into the jungle, tasting, smelling, seeing and feeling new things. Hunting was not, at first, easy: time after time Bagheera overshot his pounce and ended up wrapping his claws around a tuft of grass or his own ears. Gilhari learned the pounce faster, but it took her some time not to wake up roaring in the night, her hackles raised along her back, staring around wildly for the palace guards.

They began to know the other creatures: they learned very fast – and, in Bagheera's case, painfully – to respect the slow beauty of the elephants, and Gilhari fell in love with the sloth bears, with their clumsiness and their kindness and their fondness for fish, which, if she waited long enough, staring pointedly, they would sometimes share with her. They learned to tell the wolves apart, one from another; they learned no two animals are identical. To be alive, Bagheera found, was to be wild and various.

Bagheera found a cave for the two of them to sleep in, deep in the heart of the jungle. It was wide at the back, with a very narrow mouth that Bagheera himself could only just squeeze through. Both siblings had been raised to sleep at night and wake during the day so that they would be awake if the Royal Family wanted to

parade past and stare at them, but very slowly they began to adapt to sleeping during the heat of the sun and waking to hunt at dusk. The jungle at night shone gold and silver and deep-water blue.

In the fifth moon-cycle of their freedom, though, the jungle began to change. The sun grew hot; it seemed to swell in size until it filled the whole sky and there was no blue, only the white-hot surge of light.

The animals of the jungle grew slower; they began to trip and fall as they ran. Even the wolves, usually the most sure-footed of animals, could be seen to stumble and halt as they hunted.

Gilhari lay down in the cave and closed her eyes. "At home," she said, "they gave us clean water every day."

"Don't call it home, Gilhari," said Bagheera. "It was never home."

Gilhari butted her head against his, too exhausted to speak, and crept to the back of the cave where the air was coolest.

Bagheera hauled himself out of the cave, up from their rock, and leaped up into the trees. From there he surveyed the land.

The sun was killing the jungle. All the great green life of it was burning brown. A pack of wolves lay in the shade of a rock, too weak to reach their own cave.

As Bagheera watched, a mouse skittered over the eyelid of one of the largest wolves, who made no move, too thirsty and thin to open her jaws. To the north there was a great expanse of mud, marking what had once been a lake.

"You! Panther! Can you see a rock, there, in the middle of the pool?"

Bagheera whipped round to see who had spoken. A bear – a very old bear – sat at the foot of the tree. He was, though Bagheera did not know it then, Baloo's great-grandfather.

"Yes," said Bagheera. He was still wary of the other jungle animals, not yet knowing whom to trust, but the old bear had gentle eyes and so many flecks of white on his muzzle and back that he seemed to be almost albino. "I see it."

"Is it covered by water? Or is it dry?"

Bagheera squinted into the sun. "It's bone dry."

The bear nodded solemnly. "I thought it would be. That is Peace Rock. When the water level drops so far that Peace Rock

can be seen, the Warden of the Water calls the Water Truce."

"What truce?" Bagheera scowled, uneasy, wary of being lied to. "And what warden?"

"Hathi, the Leader of the Elephants, is Warden. And when he calls the Truce, every animal may come and drink without fear of being mauled or eaten by his next-door neighbour."

"Thank you. But why do you assume I do not already know?"

"You are new to the jungle. You need to know the Laws. The penalty for hunting anywhere here during the Truce is death."

"How do you know I am new to the jungle?" Bagheera squared his shoulders and tried to look as natural as possible, up in his tree. He rearranged his paws so that they hung over the edge of the branch, swinging casually.

"Two reasons. There has never yet been a panther as large as you, as tree-root-strong as you, as bird-fast as you. So the jungle talks. Stories spread fast here."

Bagheera tried very hard not to look pleased; he did not succeed, not even slightly.

"And you still smell of Man. Your sister – I take it she

is your sister? — moves as if she is being watched, as if she still expects to be caught."

Before Bagheera could say something rude in response, a sound rang out.

"Listen!" said the bear. "Do you hear that? That is Hathi!"

Hathi had only just taken on the chieftainship of his herd back then. His trumpet call was a little self-conscious, and spittley towards the end, but even so it rang out across the jungle, and all who were alive enough to raise their heads heard it.

"The elephants will keep the Truce," said the old bear. He sighed. "It is a hard time for them."

"Why?"

The old bear smiled. "Elephants do not relish spending time with other Jungle People; they keep to themselves. But they will set up station around the jungle to stop the tigers from tracking the deer on their way home from the watering hole."

Bagheera returned to Gilhari, full of news. Then he drew up short, some inches from the cave. A jackal had its nose in the entrance. It looked disappointed.

"Lady Panther, I will come round again in a day or two. I hope, if you are dead, you will not think it unneighbourly if I eat you."

Bagheera felt a growl rise up from his stomach to his chest to his throat. He launched through the air and landed on the jackal's back, his claws digging deep into the creature's sides.

"Say that again," he growled, "and I will tear you apart!"

The jackal writhed in his claws. "It is the way of the Jungle! It is the Law!"

"*It* is my sister," said Bagheera. "Come here again and I'll crush your head in my jaws and leave your body for the vultures."

"You cannot!" jabbered the jackal. "You cannot kill! It is the Truce! Remember the Truce!"

Bagheera unhooked his claws from the animal's flesh and batted him away. The jackal tumbled down the rock and took off as if a thousand panthers were at his back.

(The jackal insisted for the rest of his life that a stripe of his yellow-brown fur had turned white with the shock of it. Nobody believed him: jackals are not known to be truth-tellers.)

Bagheera squeezed into the cave, calling news of what the old bear had told him. Gilhari lay on her side, panting as if she had run from end to end of the jungle floor. Her ribs showed through her dark coat.

"Are you well, little sister?" asked Bagheera.

"Very well, big brother," she said, but so quietly he could barely hear her. "I heard you with the jackal. It meant no harm."

"No harm! It meant to eat you!"

"But not to kill me. When I'm dead, what will it matter?"

The words struck at Bagheera like a python. "Not *when*, Gilhari."

She smiled at him and lay her head down on the earth.

"All you need is some meat, to wake you! It's not possible to feel hopeful on an empty stomach."

She did not reply; perhaps, he thought, she was asleep.

Bagheera took off into the forest. It was as if he was possessed by the *dewanee*, the jungle madness that makes the jungle dwellers tear from tree to tree without reason or logic. He was the only fast-moving thing in sight; everything else was drained by sun and drought.

Bagheera was far into unfamiliar territory when he saw it, up high above his head on a ridge of rock: a skeleton. It had once been a buffalo, but a larger buffalo than Bagheera had ever seen. It must have slipped down the mountain and been unable to get up or down. The birds had picked the bones clean. The skull, though: Bagheera could see the skull, and the meat inside remained untouched. A bird is not strong enough to crack open a buffalo skull; the only creature that can is a tiger. Or an unusually strong panther.

Bagheera sprang at the rock, flailed for a foothold, and slid down again, his claws shrieking against the stone. He tried again, more cautiously, with the same result. There was no way up.

Bagheera rocked back on his haunches. His whole body pulsed with the need for that skull.

A vulture circled overhead. The birds – especially the kites and the vultures – suffered less painfully during the drought, for there was plenty of carrion, meat other animals could not touch without sickness. This particular vulture was positively fat, and its wingbeat was strong.

Bagheera called out to the vulture. "I need your help!" And then he added, "O my wide-winged friend!" for he was learning how the Jungle People spoke when they needed a favour. "I need that skull."

"It would take six of us a good deal of effort to get that skull down to you," said the vulture.

"I know. I would do it myself if I could."

"If you say so. But what's in it for us?" asked the vulture.

Another vulture flapped down and landed on the tree next to the first. "Yes. What will you do for us in return?"

"I'll promise you a portion of my catch for the rest of my life," said Bagheera. He ducked as a third vulture swooped down. "I will leave the juiciest portion of every animal I slay, until the day I die."

"That's not much of a promise," said the third vulture. "You look too thin to survive more than a few days."

"Then I promise you my own body when I am dead!" said Bagheera.

"We can have that anyway," said the vulture.

"No offence, I hope," said the second vulture.

"Just being practical," said the third.

Bagheera dipped his great muzzle to the ground. He closed his eyes and forced himself not to growl but to speak: "Then I promise you . . . I will break the Truce taboo and kill for you."

There was a stunned silence. The whole jungle seemed to throb and echo with his words. Then the second vulture asked, "Why not just do that now, then, and eat your kill? Why do you need us?"

"I can't. She would never eat anything killed in that way; she knows about the Truce. And I must keep her alive."

"Who?" The vultures' eyes lit up; Bagheera did not like the particular shade of enthusiasm he saw in their eyes.

"Nobody!" said Bagheera. "Nobody who has any business with you."

The vultures turned to each other and conferred, their wings hunched high over their beaks.

The first vulture turned back. "We've decided to agree," he said, "on the condition that you act fast once we've delivered the skull. Vultures do not enjoy waiting."

"Yes," said Bagheera. "Fine, anything – please, hurry!"

The second vulture gave a great squawk, and the third beat its wings in the air.

From the top of the mountain, three new dots began to appear: slowly, they spiralled down, down, to where the skeleton of the buffalo lay on the crop of rock.

The other three vultures flew up, squawking instructions to each other and clashing wings in the sky. They brushed aside the bones of the buffalo and crowded around the horns.

"Two on each horn?"

"Three on each, fool: there are six of us."

"Who are you calling a fool?"

"Concentrate, boys!" said the first vulture. "I'm hungry."

The vultures seized the horns in their talons.

"And . . . lift!" called the first vulture.

The six vultures rose, almost in unison – and the skull rose up like some great sky-monster, with a wig of twelve wings flapping above it.

The vultures flapped downward, complaining about the weight.

"Get your wing out of my beak!"

"Why's your beak open in the first place?"

They lowered the skull to Bagheera's paws. He seized it in his jaws and began to drag it, hefting it slowly over the dry-baked earth, up towards his cave. The vultures followed overhead.

He went backwards up the ridge of stone that led to the cave mouth, dragging the skull by its left horn.

"Gilhari!" he called, as he backed into the cave. "I have food! I have the most delicious food in the jungle!"

She was still asleep, lying in a pool of shadow.

"Here!" Bagheera set his jaw against the buffalo's bone. A panther has the strongest jaw of any jungle animal, but even so it was a great and painful effort to crack open the bone. At last, with a noise like a tree breaking in two, the skull broke open. The smell of meat filled the air. Bagheera took a mouthful and ran to Gilhari's side. He deposited it in front of her mouth.

"Here! Eat, little sister!"

Gilhari did not move.

"Eat!" he said more loudly. "Gilhari, I have found the only meat in the jungle for you! Eat it!"

Gilhari did not move.

"*Eat!*" he roared. "I have sworn to break the Truce of the Jungle for you! Eat it! *Eat it!*"

There was something about the way she lay, one paw under the other, that looked uncomfortable. Bagheera nudged Gilhari with his nose.

And then Bagheera rocked backwards, his whole body suddenly ice-cold in the baking heat.

Some time later – a long, dark, endless time later – the vultures waiting outside saw the black panther emerge from the cave. He carried a stone in his jaws. He placed it at the entrance.

"What are you doing?" called the first vulture.

"Why are you messing about with rocks?" called the second.

Bagheera turned on them a look of such heat and fury that all six took off in a clatter of wings.

The panther stalked down to the ground, picked up another rock in his jaws, and added it to the first. Then another, and another, until the rocks blocked the mouth of the cave entirely.

It is not the way of the jungle to bury the dead. That is a trick of Man. But Bagheera was raised among Men.

It was dawn by the time he had finished. The sun was beginning to swell to its unbearable heat again.

"You must keep your word. The Word is the Word, even from a panther to a vulture," called the first vulture. "Even the great mountain ape keeps to the Word."

Bagheera cast the bird a look of such disgust that it seemed to singe its wings.

"Keep your word," said the second vulture angrily, "or we'll knock down that wall!"

Bagheera stalked towards Peace Rock. Already, as the sun broke over the rock, the animals were gathering, the deer and the wild pigs grouped together, the old tiger and his young lame son on the opposite bank.

Bagheera watched the deer. One in particular was weaker than the others; it seemed old, and its hind leg dragged in the dirt.

He moved closer, keeping his muscles tense, ready to spring. He thought of Gilhari, of what she would say, of how her head would sink to the ground in shame.

Bagheera swallowed. He moved closer. The deer skittered, anxious, perhaps smelling his plan on his breath. Bagheera dipped his head and drank. The water tasted muddy and hot. He turned away. Two vultures flew overhead.

"Remember!" they croaked together. "Remember your promise!"

"We will not let you forget!" called the first vulture. "Vultures are good at waiting."

"I thought you said we *aren't* good at waiting?" said the second.

"I said we didn't like it, not that we can't do it," said the first.

Bagheera ignored them.

He walked without looking where he was going, with the result that he walked straight into the rock in front of him. The rock objected with a loud trumpet that shook the trees above them.

"Watch where you're going!" said the elephant.

Bagheera stared up at her, dazed, but did not apologize.

"I know who you are," said the elephant.

The elephant was young then, almost as young as Bagheera, though at the time Bagheera was not a good estimator of elephant age. And he would not have cared.

"Fine," said Bagheera.

"I know who you are," the elephant said again, "and I know what you're about to do."

"Do you?" asked Bagheera. "Then you know more than I do.

I do not know what I'm going to do at all."

The elephant bent her knees so that her head was nearer to Bagheera's. She was very young, or she would not have done anything so compromising of her dignity, but there was something in the panther's eyes that made her great grey body ache. She could see his heart shake inside him as he stood.

"I have an idea," she said.

"I have no use for ideas," said Bagheera.

"I have a secret. I was going to tell the Wolf Pack, but instead I'll tell you."

Bagheera did not say, "What?" He simply looked at her: at the thick, wrinkled skin across her trunk, changing to leaf-thin at the tips of her ears. She was barely more than a child then, and her black eyes were brighter than they are now.

"I found a wild pig, down by the purple flowering trees." The elephant waited, but Bagheera said nothing. "It's dead. It died of the sun."

"Why are you telling me? It's too late! It's too late to help her!"

"You can run there now, before the vultures see – and slit its throat – and – and cover yourself in blood a little – and they will think you have done what you promised. And then – then you won't have to break the Truce!"

"What difference does it make?"

"What?"

"Everyone will think I have broken the Truce anyway."

"But *you* will know!" she said. "That will matter. It is what a creature such as Gilhari would have done."

Bagheera jerked backwards and his hackles rose along his back; he bared his teeth at the elephant, as if, despite her vast size, he would bite her in two.

"How do you know her name?" he said.

"I know far more about her than her name. Elephants hear all the stories of the jungle, and they are not permitted to forget them, else they would slip out of the world like water. We know about the ancient white ape living in the mountains, and the blind snakes under the rocks, and the names of every animal to die in our territory. It is our way," she said. She felt old, suddenly, thinking of it. "We pass the Laws and the stories down. We have no human writing, so we etch them in the mind of the next generation. We are many. Even if one forgets, there will be enough to remember. Go, now, before somebody else finds it."

Bagheera moved as if he was half asleep. With a bitter taste on his tongue, he did as he was bid. He found the boar under the shade of the tree and tore open its throat. But Bagheera did not allow himself a single bite: he merely tore at the chest to make it look as if it were a true kill, and then he crouched over the boar and called for the vultures.

He waited until the vultures were feasting, and then he turned his back and stalked away. He went slowly, looking neither up nor down, towards the place where the jungle grows so thickly that night and day are inseparable.

The Jungle Folk did not come after him to seek recompense for breaking the Truce. It is possible the elephant told them. Or it is possible that they simply understood.

But Bagheera neither knew nor cared. He grew wilder and wilder.

As time went on, the young animals pointed him out to one another in awe.

"That's Bagheera," they would whisper.

"His whiskers are steel and his muscles are iron . . ."

"And he walks by his wild lone."

Bagheera grew more terrible in the jungle than Shere Khan. He feared nothing, for he had nothing to lose: he did not fear the tigers, nor the bitter white ape who files his claws to thorn-points each night. He did not even fear the drought.

He grew sharp-toothed and fierce even to those who would have gladly been his friend, and he did not take the risk of love again.

At least, not until a scrap of a man-child appeared, quick-footed as a squirrel and black-haired as a panther, one very warm evening in the Seoni hills.'

Baloo's Courage

Mowgli sat with his chin on his knees, his back against the elephant's foot, stunned into stillness.

'Bagheera never told me he had a sister!' he said. 'I tell him *everything*.'

'He tells very few things to very few people,' said Rapi. 'It is his way.'

'And the elephant,' said Mowgli. 'That was . . . that was you, wasn't it?'

Rapi ran the tip of her trunk through Mowgli's shock of hair.

'Perhaps, little frog. Now, tell me, how are your lessons?'

Mowgli was just opening his mouth to reply when he heard a rustling in the undergrowth. He sniffed the air. It was unmistakably his mother. Raksha was moving fast, and there was a smell in the air of fury – or fear.

All thoughts of Bagheera disappeared. Mowgli grabbed a vine in both fists and began to shin up it. He pumped his legs back and forth to make it swing, then launched himself towards another, higher vine. He made a hurried salute to Rapi as he tumbled through the air; then he grabbed the vine in both hands and disappeared into the safety of the leaves.

Far, far above, high on a rock above the canopy, a pair of red eyes watched him go.

One hour later, the great bear Baloo was sitting by the river, teaching the youngest litter of wolf cubs a lesson in Rat, when Mowgli crashed down from the green curtain overhead. He landed, panting, at the bear's paws, and butted Baloo in his furry stomach.

'Come and play, old bear!' he said. 'I've got stories to tell you.'

Baloo gently batted Mowgli away with the side of his head. 'I'm teaching. Come and join the lesson, Mowgli, or leave us be for now.'

'I'll join the lesson.' Mowgli was in a strutting, peacocking mood. 'I can show them how it's done!'

'Very well,' said Baloo. 'Mowgli, how do you say "I am grateful for your help" in Rat?'

'Why would I ever have to say that?' Mowgli laughed. 'When are the rats ever going to help me?'

Without warning, Baloo's vast, rough-padded paw swept out and knocked Mowgli across the chest. Mowgli was bowled backwards, heels over head, and lay in the dirt looking up at the treetops. They were spinning.

He scrambled to his feet, unhurt but furious. 'What was that for?' he asked. 'What did I do?'

'By the great ape, wolfling, the Words of the Jungle are not a subject to joke about! I do not teach for my own amusement; I teach because it matters more than anything else.'

'You didn't have to hit me!' said Mowgli.

But Baloo merely turned his great back and went on teaching the younger wolves.

As Mowgli stood, spitting rage and humiliation and dirt, Akela stepped out of the grass. He had been watching the cubs as they learned; it is a Pack Leader's job to know the strengths and fooleries of every newborn wolf.

'Come with me, man-child. Leave the cubs.'

Mowgli dusted himself off, and turned his nose up at the old bear's back. 'I'm going with Akela,' said Mowgli loudly. 'We're going to discuss important things, without you.'

Akela did not turn round to look at the boy, merely led the way to the Council Rock. Akela was growing white around the eyes and muzzle, and he grew leaner by the year; his spine rose and fell like a mountain range as he prowled onward.

Mowgli's blood was still hot and itchy in his veins, but by the time they reached the Rock, his rage had abated just enough for him to swing up into the trees for a clutch of bananas. He glanced down to make sure Akela was watching, and then turned a few somersaults, to show he was unconcerned.

Far above on the outcrop of rock, the red eyes took note of the speed of the man-cub's limbs and the wild whip of his head as he spun in mid-air, knees tucked tight against his chest, unaware of being watched.

Mowgli shimmied down the tree again, peeled a banana with his toes, and ate it in two still-slightly-grumpy mouthfuls.

Akela waited until the boy stopped huffing and fell still. 'Did anyone ever tell you,' he asked, 'about how Baloo came to be your teacher? About how he came to be the guide of all the young cubs, in fact, of all the jungle?'

'No.' Mowgli picked a tick out of the crook of his elbow and bit it defiantly. 'And I don't care about that stupid old bear.'

'It's a story worth hearing,' said Akela.

There was something flinty in the old wolf's eyes: something that said it would be better not to refuse. 'Fine.' Mowgli peeled another banana and lay on his back, looking up at the wolf's muzzle. 'Tell me,' he said.

Akela lay down on the hot rock and scratched himself luxuriously with his hind leg.

'This story begins when Baloo was a fairly small and very fluffy cub. Baloo was not, by any stretch of the imagination, an elegant bear,' said Akela. 'He was larger than his brothers; round-eyed, and slow-pawed, and clumsy. He shed fur everywhere. He was un-nervous and unwary, lax and slack and the kind to eat his own toenails.

'The other bears were not very patient with him.

Baloo was not a peaceful cave-companion. Even as a newborn cub, before he first opened his eyes, he snuffled and sang and imitated the sounds around him. He mimicked the voice of the red parrot and the green. He copied the snores of his father and the grunts of his siblings as they ate.

"Baloo!" his mother would say. "Will you be quiet, before I bite my own whiskers off!"

"Quiet!" his father would roar, his fur standing on end with exhaustion. "Or we'll send you off to the ancient ape up the mountain! We're trying to sleep!"

Nobody noticed how perfectly Baloo's snores and hoots were pitched, how very closely they matched the original.

By the time he was a year old, Baloo was a ball of fur who chewed his claws and played on his own.

The other cubs did not mean to be cruel, exactly, but nor did they mean to be kind. Baloo was liable to mistime his happiness and barge into the other cubs while they were eating and, when they groomed one another, he bit too hard.

One bright morning at the foot of the Seoni hills, three of Baloo's cousins and two of his brothers were playing outside the cave. The game involved running in circles and trying to catch the stumpy tail of the bear in front of you. Baloo woke and heard the joyful growls coming from outside. He came galloping out of the cave and threw himself into the circle. He caught his left front claw under a root and went headlong into the bear in front, who crashed into his cousin in front of him. The bears rolled in a pile of fur and teeth. There was a certain amount of spitting.

"Baloo!"

"Ow, don't – that's my nose!"

"Sorry!" said Baloo. "Sorry, sorry."

Baloo's brother Ors rolled his top lip back to show his teeth. "Baloo would find a way to trip over his own paws even if he was a *fish*."

The cubs laughed and stamped their hind legs on the ground.

Baloo's face creased. "Fish don't have paws," he said.

Ors sighed. "I *know*. That's why it's *funny*."

Baloo sat up and tried to nonchalantly extract some leaf-mould from his eye. "I'd still like to play," he said. "If you explain the rules?"

"No! We're busy."

"Just go. Go home."

Baloo looked around the clearing. "This *is* my home."

"Then go somewhere else."

Baloo laughed uncertainly. "You're joking?"

"We're not," said Ors. "Leave us alone."

When you are told to leave someone alone, Baloo discovered, the person who invariably feels most alone is you. Baloo tried to look jaunty as he set off through the green jungle, but his heart was so low he was sure he could feel it dragging on the forest floor.

He tugged his heart and legs along until he found a large rock in a clearing. It had trapped the warmth of the sun in its grey embrace. He lay down with his back against it and closed his eyes.

Then he opened them. Something was trying to eat his eyebrows.

He scrambled up and rose on his hind legs, trying to look ferocious. He bared his teeth and stared around at the sky, then into the trees, then down at the ground. A very small creature was staring up at him.

Baloo didn't pay much attention to any animal that wasn't at least as big as his own head. This creature would barely cover a quarter of his forepaw.

It had the face and body of a mouse but with over-size back legs, like a rabbit's, which allowed it to jump as high as a grown human's waist. It had vast ears, waving like an elephant's in the breeze. A jerboa, Baloo thought. He'd seen a few near the lake, though none had ever tried to chew at his fur before.

It squeaked. Baloo blinked.

"I don't understand," he said.

It is important to remember that back in the years Baloo was young, the large animals of the jungle did not speak the languages of the smaller. Most bears could speak Wolf, Tiger, Panther, Elephant, but anything else they regarded as nonsense. "Hideous squeaking," they would say. "Makes my ears ache."

Likewise, the smaller mammals – the mice and rats and squirrels – did not learn Tiger or Wolf. This was largely because they didn't have the chance to get close enough without being eaten.

So Baloo stared at the jerboa. It squeaked again. Its tiny eyes looked kind. And Baloo found himself more than usually in need of kindness that day.

So Baloo squeaked back. He tried to imitate the exact squeak of the jerboa.

The jerboa squeaked again – this time it was clear that she was laughing. She turned and squeaked into the bushes nearby, and three more jerboas appeared, their ears flapping inquisitively.

Baloo tried the jerboa squeak again. Although he did not know it at the time, his squeak was not an accurate one. As in all languages, there are words in Jerboa that sound very similar but mean very different things. The jerboa had said, "Hello! What's wrong?"

Baloo had said, "Constipation! What's smelling?"

But it was a beginning. And a beginning is a precious thing, as delicate and fragile as a newborn starling.

The jerboa gestured at herself, and then at Baloo, and tipped her head to one side in the way that means, in every language, both animal and human, "What are you called?"

Baloo growled his name. As best she could, the jerboa growled it back. Bear is a fairly simple language, so her effort wasn't in fact that bad.

"Boola," she growled. The growl was so high-pitched and foreign that Baloo wanted to laugh, but he contained himself.

He pointed at the jerboa.

"Jolt," she said.

"Joolt," said Baloo. He pointed at a nearby stone. "Rock," he growled.

"Rockkk," the jerboas squeaked in Bear.

Baloo pointed at the rock again, and then at the jerboas, and raised his eyebrows in a question.

"Rock!" they squeaked in Jerboa.

Baloo tried to raise his voice to a squeak. "Orck," he growled. "Orrrck."

The jerboas thumped their feet in applause. Baloo smiled. He felt something prickle on his tongue. It was, he thought, language, struggling to be born. Or possibly a stray ant.

❧

Baloo went every day to the clearing, wading when it rained through mud that came up to his knees. The language took weeks to arrive. But although he was slow-pawed and clumsy, Baloo was not, it turned out, slow-witted. As the rains gave way to sun, Baloo gathered up thousands of Jerboa words. He seemed to eat the words alive, such was his hunger for them. It was an extraordinary scene, had anyone been there to witness it: quivering, delicate squeaks emitting from the mouth of a

five-foot ball of black fur and teeth.

One morning, when the sun felt hot enough to burn holes in his skin, Baloo looked around for a spring. "I wish to be watered," he said in Jerboa. "My mouth-snake is dry," he said, waggling his tongue.

There was some consulting among the jerboas. Jolt seemed to be arguing with the others; Baloo could only catch a few words — among them, "secret" and "clumsy". Jolt, though, was nearly two years old — a full year older than Baloo — and she glared at her younger siblings until they fell silent.

"They say, *Do you swear not to tell where we take you?*" asked Jolt.

"I swoor," said Baloo. And, in Bear, "May the ancient ape come for me if I lie."

Jolt led Baloo down into the places where the jungle grew thickest, where Baloo had to bite and claw himself a path through the undergrowth.

"There!" she said.

At Baloo's feet there was a hidden spring, which rose from

between rocks to form a pool of bright water. Dragonflies flitted around his head, their wings burring in his ears and ruffling his fur with their miniature breeze.

It was there that Baloo began to learn languages in earnest.

The jerboa mentioned him to the brown mice, who came to stare at him as he counted to a hundred in Jerboa. Then there were the Gairdner's shrewmice, with their long noses and cropped fur that brushed soft against Baloo's paws. The shrewmice introduced Baloo to the Brahma white-bellied rats, with the splash of white fur tucked under their chins. There were the palm squirrels, with the black and white stripes down their backs, their voices as high as a cricket's.

More and more, Baloo found himself spending time away from the cave, down by the spring in the heart of the dense undergrowth.

He would find his way there alone, checking over his shoulder to make sure he wasn't being followed by his brothers, and then he would set back his head and call, in Jerboa, "Come, come, come, come, *come*!" (He still pronounced it "coomb", but the jerboas were too polite to mention it.)

Jolt and her siblings would come tumbling and jumping through the grass, and they would play.

Some games were less easy than others. Hide-and-seek was, as Baloo protested, extremely unfair. Baloo and Jolt and the rats could race – size wasn't necessarily an advantage in the thickly twined heart of the jungle – but Baloo had to make sure not to step on his opponents, and it was all rather more stressful than was ideal.

They tried to groom one another, which was more successful, although when Baloo tried to groom the smaller mice, there was a risk that he would lick off their fur along with the grass and leaves.

In return the mice and jerboas would swarm all over Baloo, nibbling at any bits of greenery or insects that had got caught in his fur. It tickled and made him kick and wriggle as he lay on his stomach.

All the while, Baloo would practise his new tongues. It wasn't easy. He mixed up the languages, and spoke Rat to the mice, Jerboa to the squirrels. In Pangolin he tried to say, "Please could I have an ant?" and in fact said, "Please can I chew on your aunt?"

which led to misunderstandings.

Baloo persevered. "Will I climb the brown flower to bring down the bee-spit?" he would squeak, pointing at a great spreading oak and the honeycomb far over his head. "See the wet-sky!" he would exclaim, pointing at the lake. "Let us swoomb."

Slowly, word by word, day by day, he got better. He barely noticed the first time he answered a question in Jerboa without thinking. Instead of translating the word into Bear, thinking of an answer, and translating that back into Jerboa, he answered automatically. "Yes, ravenous," he said. "Let's find something to eat."

Learning Rat took the longest. This was because jungle rats are so polite that it's almost impossible to understand them. Do not start a conversation with a rat unless you have an afternoon to spare: it takes them half an hour to convey the most basic thought. Once, Baloo came across a cluster of rats who had found a long-dead body of a deer.

"Would you please to taste the first morsel of the flesh of the delectable decaying carcass laid out by providence before us?" asked the first rat.

"After you!" replied a second. "The first mouthful is the most toothsome! I would not dream of impinging on that which is rightfully yours!"

Baloo watched with wide eyes. It seemed they would starve to death before either stopped talking.

Rats have an unfairly poor reputation. They are, in fact, fair-minded and elegant. As any rat would tell you if you gave them a chance, they might indeed eat your face, but only if you were dead already, which is more than you can say for the tigers and the wolves. What is a scavenger, really, but an animal with a tidy mind?

Once, one of the rats came to the mouth of the cave to call for Baloo. Before he could do more than utter his first "By your leave, honourable midnight-coated squire of the jungle," he was chased away by Baloo's father, Pita.

Pita was taller than any other bear in the jungle. His front paws were calloused and scarred from warning other bears away. For sheer weight and heft, he was a marvel. But his bones ached, and his joints were audible. He could feel age clawing at him. He had lost a great chunk of fur from behind his shoulders in a fight with a tiger, and when he walked down the mountain these days, it was slowly, searching out his footing like an uncertain cub.

"What was he doing here?" Pita asked Baloo. There was anger in his voice, just below the surface. "They should know not to come near us."

"Why?" said Baloo.

"Rats are filthy!" said Pita. "They eat poo."

"They don't! *Some* rats eat *near* poo. There's a difference."

Pita huffed so powerfully that a hair ball shot out of his mouth and hit Baloo on the ear. "Nonsense," he said. "They're beneath you."

Baloo opened his mouth, but Pita broke in.

"I know. I know what you think of me: you think I am cruel. But it is the Way of the Jungle. Never be friends with anything you could accidentally sit on. Stay with the other cubs."

"But the other cubs don't like me!"

"Then *make* them like you! Learn to play the games they like."

"Even if I could, they wouldn't want me."

"I don't care what they want. They're cubs. Cubs do what they're told."

"I can't tell them to like me! It doesn't work," Baloo said. "I've tried."

Baloo's father sighed. "Oh, go away and eat something, child."

"I can't," said Baloo. "All the ant mounds round here are too thick to break into."

Pita sighed deeply and took Baloo out to an ant mound. He held out his claws to Baloo. They curved inwards, each as long as a fish, and they shone bone-white in the light. "This is what a claw should look like."

Baloo looked at his own claws. He chewed them in his sleep, and they were ragged-edged and blunt. He gave an experimental swipe at an anthill. A few flakes of dirt came away. He tried again, and his claw went halfway into the thick red mud of the mound and got stuck.

The ants seemed to be laughing.

Baloo stifled a mew of disappointment. *Bears do not mew*, he told himself.

Pita sighed again. He gathered his strength and gave a great swipe at the nest. But he stumbled on his left hind leg as he did so, and his paw missed the anthill and swept in a full circle, smacking against his own back. To a stranger it would have looked funny; except it was not, not at all, not even slightly.

Baloo looked away immediately so as not to meet his father's eye.

Pita let out a grunt that was close to a roar. He pulled back his front leg and with one great jab tore open a hole in the ants' nest.

Baloo fell on the nest with happy grunts. He was not a tidy eater, and ants flew everywhere, down his front and into his ears. Eventually, though, he caught his father's eye and stepped hurriedly aside.

Carefully Pita blew away the dust, then began to suck out

the insects through the gap in his front teeth. He had to close his nostrils to do so, and form his lips like a hollow straw, which made it difficult to talk.

"*Oh back to the ave*," he told Baloo.

"What?"

Pita flared his nostrils and drew in breath. "*Go* back to the *cave*, cub," he repeated. "I don't wish to be stared at while I eat. Don't you understand Bear when you hear it?"

Baloo retreated to the cave and stayed there, licking his paws and fuming. He *did* understand Bear; he spoke it better than almost anyone, and he spoke three dozen other languages besides. The world was unfair and unhinged.

It was that night that the news came. It changed everything.

He was lying wide awake in the cave, listening to the snoring of his brothers and mother, when the kite sounded the alarm. But it was Jolt who first heard it and came sprinting to find Baloo.

She darted into the cave and shouted. A jerboa's shout is not very loud, and the bears snored on. She edged further into the cave and chewed on the cub's ear.

"Baloo! Baloo! Wake up!"

"What?" Baloo sat bolt upright. "Jolt!"

"Is that a mouse? Speaking Bear?" asked his mother, Janani.

"I'm a jerboa," said Jolt. "But yes, I speak Bear."

"I taught her," said Baloo.

"And I taught him Jerboa," said Jolt proudly.

Baloo saw Janani's eyes widen in horror, and he turned his back on his family, crouching low over Jolt, protective and urgent.

"What is it? Why are you here?"

"The kite! He has something to tell you!"

"What?"

"I can't tell exactly what he's saying – but I knew the words for 'bear' and your name. Quickly! He's outside!"

Baloo lolloped to the mouth of the cave and looked out. Kite circled high overhead, but at the sight of the bear cub, he swooped low and landed on a branch.

Kites eat jerboas. Jolt was quaking, one eye on the bird

overhead, one eye on the bears inside the cave. But Kite was not interested in feeding.

"Bears!" he called. "Bears, all of you, come forth! Your father is taken!"

"My father?" Baloo stared at him blankly. "Taken where? Taken unwell?"

"No! Taken by the human pack!"

"He can't have been!" said Baloo. "He was with me at the ants' nest only a few hours ago! He can't have—"

"Hush, child." Janani came to the mouth of the cave, surrounded by her cubs, and looked up at the bird. "You must be wrong. We harm neither the cattle nor the children of men. They've no cause to hate us. Surely it was a wolf they took?"

Kite glared. A kite's eyebrows always, even when they are at their most cheerful, look a little accusatory. A kite's glare is twice as painful as any other creature's.

"I was not mistaken. They came with ropes. They bound his claws and mouth and tied him to a branch and carried him away on their shoulders."

"They can't have!" said Baloo. "You've made a mistake."

But Janani's eyes had changed; they were suddenly as dark as the heart of the Earth. "Alive?" she asked. "Or dead?"

"Alive. He roared so loud the leaves above unfastened themselves and fell on the heads of the humans as they ran back to the village."

"Did you follow?" said Janani. "Did you see where they went?"

Kite bowed his head. "It's not good news."

"Tell me!"

"They took him to the village."

"To one of their brick-caves?"

"No. No, he is too big to fit through the doorway. They have a pit, dug twice as deep as a bear's height. He is there, barely able to take three steps in any direction. They have bound his front paws, to make him walk on his hind legs."

Baloo shivered with horror. "Are you sure?"

"I wish that I was not, little cub. I'm sorry."

"What are they going to do with him?" he asked. "Will they eat him?"

"No," said Kite. "It will be worse. I've seen such things before. Send your cubs back into the cave. This is not for their ears."

A single look from Janani, and the cubs retreated. But Baloo waited only a second and then crept back to the mouth of the cave, crouching in shadow to listen.

Kite spoke very softly. "You know what they will do, Janani. They will make him dance."

Baloo let out a bark so full of incredulity and panic that it sounded almost like laughter.

Janani turned to him. "I told you to go back to sleep, Baloo," she said. But all the fight had left her voice. Her very spine seemed to have become curved and weak.

"You can't *force* a bear to dance!" said Baloo. "It's impossible! It would be like forcing a bear to . . . to tell a story, or to fall in love."

But Janani shook her head. Her muzzle almost touched the earth, and her voice was very low. "It's not impossible, child. I've heard of it. They cannot make a bear dance, but they can force us to do something that looks to humans like dancing."

"How?"

"With canes and whips. With pins and fire."

"Then we have to get him back!"

Janani and Kite exchanged looks: looks filled with the sadness that had grown over years like an oak tree rising. Baloo did not like that look.

Kite shook his head. "They'll be keeping a lookout, in case he manages to escape, and they'll have death sticks with them."

"He means guns," said Janani.

"I don't care! I'll go!"

"You!" said Kite. "You haven't lost your first-year fluff, cub."

"He's my father!"

"That's brave," said the kite; it did not sound entirely like a compliment. "But no matter how brave you are, you cannot face a bullet from one of those sticks and live."

"I'm small! They might not be able to hit me! I'll dodge and dance! I'll get in the pit and bite through the rope that binds him, and we'll run home!"

"You are not so small as all that, little one," said Kite.

"Go, child, and sleep," said Janani.

"I'm not tired! We need to go and get Father!"

"Then go and find something to eat," said Janani. "I need to talk to Kite alone."

Baloo stared at her imploringly, but she batted him away with her nose and turned her back. Half blind with confusion and misery, he stumbled away down the slope towards the stream. Jolt followed.

She did not speak until Baloo had dipped his head to the water and taken a long drink, cool water calming the hot misery in his nose and ears.

"Baloo? You heard how the kite said you're not small enough to dodge a bullet?"

"Yes." Baloo pawed at the dirt. "I know."

"But, Baloo?"

"Yes?"

"I am."

❖

Hours later, Baloo sat rubbing his back nervously against a mango tree, surrounded by jerboas. Jolt had summoned her family – her sisters, and brothers, and eighth cousins twelve times removed – and they crouched in a cluster looking up at Baloo, their ears twitching in the sun. Some of the younger jerboas were so young and small, he could have balanced them on the edge of his claw. There was a rat too, and a smattering of brown mice.

Jolt ran up Baloo's back and perched on his shoulder, looking down at the jerboas. "I called you," she began, "because I need your help. A bear has been taken by the human village. Baloo needs to get him back. And we can help!"

"Why should we?" asked one of the more belligerent jerboas. "What have the bears ever done for us? Except teach us how to speak Bear – and we taught them Jerboa, so it's even."

"Baloo is my friend, Jin," said Jolt simply. She seemed to expect it to be more convincing than it was.

"He's not *my* friend," said Jin. "I repeat my question: What have the bears ever done for us?"

Jolt whipped her head around, her ears vibrating with anger. "And what if the answer was *nothing*? What if they'd never even looked in our direction?" she said. "But what if we needed help? And they said, '*What have the jerboas ever done for us?*' Each species would wait for the other to begin, until we were all bones on the jungle floor." She looked around at the sea of waving ears and twitching whiskers below her. "We can't wait for the other one to begin in kindness."

Jin looked fixedly at a spot several inches above Jolt's ear. "Fine," he muttered. "I was only asking."

"But we have a problem," said Jolt. "Baloo and I have a plan. But the plan needs more of us. How many more can we gather? Jolyn?"

The oldest jerboa looked around and shook her head. "I think this is all of us. The rest are not on speaking terms."

"Then we'll need other rodents. Who here speaks Rat?"

Most of the jerboas nodded. Baloo raised his paw.

"And Mouse?"

"Of course!"

"And Shrewmouse?"

There was a silence. Then: "I do," piped up Jin. "A bit."

"Jin!" said Jolyn. "You shouldn't be associating with the shrewmice!"

"This is so absolutely, entirely, not the time for this! Don't you see? We need one another!" said Jolt. She turned to Jin. "Do you know their Words – their emergency call?"

Jin nodded.

"Good. Then we must have a summoning. At dusk – to catch both the day- and night-dwellers. Who else?"

"The squirrels. And the moles! They're brave."

"They're not brave. They're short-sighted. They can't see danger coming, that's all."

"Call the moles!" said Jolt. "Call anyone you can think of. Anyone fast and small."

"Thank you," said Baloo. "I can't thank you enough."

"There's just one small problem," said Jin.

"Yes?"

"You never actually told us the plan."

Baloo and Jolt exchanged a glance. Baloo tried to hide his nerves.

"It might not work," he began, "but—"

"Don't say that!" hissed Jolt. "That's not how you rally an army!"

"Oh. In that case, it will definitely work," said Baloo.

"Sound more certain! Sound like you've done it a thousand times before!"

"The plan," said Baloo – and, though he felt deeply foolish, he reared up, slashed his paws in the air and arranged his face to look battle-ready – "is Jolt's, and it is the best plan I've ever heard!"

"Yes, fine, but what *is* it?" asked Jin.

Baloo stopped waving his paws. "The plan is: We swarm the village."

"Swarm?"

"Yes!" said Jolt. She jumped from foot to foot in excitement, ruffling Baloo's fur. "Like bees."

"We're jerboas. We can't fly," said Jin. "Or had you not noticed?

The ears are ornamental. They don't flap."

"OK, not a swarm. A *wave* of us," said Jolt. "A sea of rodents! And if they shoot at us, even if they hit us, there will be thousands more."

"*Shoot* at us?" said Jin.

"And then," said Baloo, "you find the pit and bite through my father's bindings."

"And he'll climb out on our backs and we'll run."

"Climb out *on our backs*?" said Jin. "Can you hear yourself talking?"

"On the backs of hundreds and hundreds of us! Together, we'll be more than strong enough."

"And what's to stop them just shooting him as he escapes?"

"We thought of that. We need something that will terrify them. So they won't be able to move a single finger. Something they have never seen before."

"How are we going to do that? I mean, everyone's seen a rat." He turned to the rat. "No offence meant."

"None taken, my large-eared comrade."

"We thought," said Jolt, "what if we dyed ourselves a different colour?"

Jolt paused for a murmur of excitement. The silence was so total, Baloo could hear the jerboas' ears flapping in the breeze.

"What if we were bright yellow? Yellow rats, yellow mice? What if it looked like the sky was leaking down? What if it looked like the sun itself was seeking vengeance?"

"And how exactly do you plan to dye us yellow?" said Jolyn.

"It's easier than you think," said Baloo.

"We do the call tonight," said Jolt. She twitched her whiskers authoritatively. "And tomorrow, we'll show you what to do."

That night in the jungle, an extraordinary noise went forth. The jerboas ran through the undergrowth, giving forth the call of the rats, of the mice. The rats called for the squirrels; the mice called out for the voles. The whole jungle rang with a wild squeaking.

But it seemed to Baloo as he lay listening that the loudest noise of all, as he lay curled in a corner of the cave, was the beating of his own terrified heart.

Baloo remembered facts only if they were about food. He could not recite his own family tree, which bears are supposed to be able to do for all living generations, up to fifth cousins. (The law was designed to stop families accidentally killing each other, but Baloo was confident he wasn't going to be murdering anybody any day soon. It just wasn't his kind of thing.)

But Baloo could recall exactly where the best black ants were to be found, where the sharp, spicy red ants could be unearthed, where the salty tang of termites could be pulled down from a tree. He could remember the exact location of every honey-bee hive in the jungle. And he knew where to find the lichen that made a delicious after-ant mouth-cleanser.

Early that morning, Baloo led the crowd of jerboas, rats, mice and squirrels to a vast side of rock that stretched across the floor for a thousand paces, spotted and coated with lichen. Baloo clawed at the lichen; the mice scrabbled at it, their claws scratching with a shrieking so shrill it could be heard across the jungle.

Baloo filled his jaws with lichen until it leaked out down his chin. He mulched the lichen in his teeth. "To release the colour," he said with his mouth full.

"We'll smell of bear spit!" said one of the shrewmice.

Baloo's face creased. He stopped chewing.

Jolt shoved at the shrewmouse with her nose. "That's a perfectly pleasant thing to smell of. At least his mouth is clean – unlike yours. You've got something brown caught in your front teeth."

Baloo spat out the lichen carefully on to the ground. "Now you roll in it," he said.

Jolt marched forward, then leaped into it, as if diving into a pool. She emerged spotted and striped in yellow, with a startlingly bright patch on her head.

"Did it work?" she asked, twisting to look. Her tail was bright sun-colour, and her ears were stained ochre.

"You look like a tiny tiger," said Baloo.

"Not all that tiny," she said sternly. She twirled her tail in the air, attempting to get a proper look at it. "I'm actually rather tall for my age."

Two hours later, they were ready. It felt like commanding an army: an army that came up no higher than Baloo's knee. Every single animal was dyed bright yellow: it was as if a field of marigolds had grown whiskers and legs.

Baloo stood at the edge of the jungle, looking down the earthen path towards the human village. There was a circle of houses, some barns, an area where children were playing with a ball, and, at the edge of the village, a deep hole dug in the ground. From the hole, terrible noises were arising: the roar of a humiliated and raging old bear.

Baloo felt his breath stutter in his throat. He looked down at the crusade ranged at his feet. Jolt looked up at him. Baloo gave the smallest of nods.

Jolt cleared her throat. "I can't promise you," she began,

"that nobody will die today."

"Good start," muttered Jin.

"But I *can* promise," she went on, "that today, if we fight, we can change everything. I can promise that we will show the jungle that we are many, that a mouse can be as fierce as a wolf, and that a rat is the equal of a tiger. And we can save the life of the father of my dearest and largest friend. What other bear would bother to learn our ways, our language? What other bear has loved us so truly? For Baloo!" she cried.

And the cry went up, in Shrew and Mouse and Squirrel. "For Baloo! For Baloo, Baloo, Baloo!"

"For our even-tempered and intellectually curious ally, Baloo!" cried the rats. "Let this day be a memorial of our—"

And then the sea surged forward and the rats had to stop squeaking to run, and they coursed down the path, kicking up red dust that spotted and striped their yellow backs, squeaking and peeping and roaring.

Baloo stayed where he was. He had promised not to follow. "You are not small enough to dodge a bullet," Jolt had said. "That's the *whole point*."

Baloo could not bear to look away: he stared, open-jawed, at the scores upon scores of rodents as they ran, with Jolt at their head, her ears streaming behind her like a battle flag.

The jerboas led the way, shining fierce yellow in the sun, towards the hole. A shout came from the village, and a horde of small children came tearing out of the houses to stare, followed by their mothers and fathers.

"Get back!" one of the men cried. "Fetch the guns!"

"But what is it?"

"I don't know! Whatever it is, we need guns!"

The sea of rodents grew closer to the bear pit. The men disappeared and reappeared, running, with their weapons. The sea of rodents reached the hole and began to pour into it.

"It's . . . rats! And mice!"

"It's not! It can't be!"

"They're yellow!"

"And when have you seen a rat and a mouse and a squirrel together?"

"Don't shoot! It's something uncanny!"

Jolt threw herself, head and front paws first, down into the hole. Inside, there was loose dirt and a few chewed bones and a roaring, furious bear.

One of his front paws was bleeding where he had tried to bite off the rope. He stared at Jolt.

"Who are you? What's happening?"

Jolt spoke in Bear. "Baloo sent me. We've come to get you out.

Everything's going to be all right."

The old bear's face was very bitter. "Nothing is all right. And if anyone were able to make it so, it would not be Baloo."

As they spoke, dozens more jerboas began to swarm into the hole, followed by the rats, the mice, the sea of squirrels and voles, and three overexcited mongooses.

"What is this?" cried the old bear. "What are they doing here?"

Jolt ignored him. She called an order to her troops. The rodents pushed aside the astonished bear and began to dig into the earth, scooping it out with their claws and making indents in the earth

walls, two tall columns of holes, spaced a bear's leg-length apart. It was hard going: the earth was as unyielding as rock, and the mice were quaking with nerves. When they had dug the lower holes, they reached higher, balancing on each other's backs eight-deep to reach high enough.

Jolt turned urgently to the bear. "Hold out your paws," she said, and she began to chew through the ropes, her teeth catching on their rough fibre, spitting out strands of it as she worked desperately to release him. At last the rope began to thin and fray.

"Pull!" said Jolt.

The bear heaved his paws apart. The rope strained but did not break.

"Harder!" said Jolt.

"I am tired," said Pita. His muzzle dropped to his chest. "I am so tired. Leave me."

"I don't care!" Jolt ran up the bear's back and stood on the edge of his nose, her whiskers vibrating with fury. "Baloo has summoned half the jungle to save you! I don't care about you, but I care about him, and his heart is conjoined to yours. Now pull! *Pull!*"

The ropes snapped and flew into the dirt. Pita stared around him at the lake of rodents skittering over him, as if seeing them for the first time.

"What in the name of all the bees in Seoni—" began the bear.

"Climb out!" cried Jolt. "You use the holes for steps!"

The bear looked at the holes, then at his injured paw. "How?" he said. "I appreciate your efforts. But . . . impossible."

"We'll push you from behind. Don't argue! Out, before they decide to shoot!"

The rats and mice began to swarm behind the bear, climbing on one another's bodies, their claws in each other's eyes and noses, heaving their backs against the bear. Slowly, with a great roar, Pita rose from the hole.

"Look!" One man cocked his gun. "The bear's escaping!"

But before he could shoot, Jolt gave a shrill roar. "Attack!"

Half the yellow army peeled off and headed straight for the men. Their tiny teeth were bared, and they left a yellow trail over the earth as they went.

"What the—" cried one of the men.

"What *are* they?" shouted another.

One of the rats leaped towards the man's ankles. The man swung his rifle down and fired. The rat flew upward and then fell, motionless, to the ground.

There was a short, sharp silence. The other rats stared, silent for the first time in their lives. And then: "Attack!" cried Jin. "Attack!" And he sprang over the heads of the other rodents and straight at the crotch of the man.

"For our fallen brother!" cried the rats. "For our comrade!" They launched themselves at the men's legs, biting and spitting.

"Run!" screamed the man.

"Faster! I can feel their teeth at my ankles!"

The men turned and ran, covering their heads and eyes with their hands against the sudden onslaught of teeth, sprinting back towards the safety of their homes.

The day looked won. The army turned and began to stream back to the jungle. The old bear began to lope painfully up the dirt path towards the jungle, surrounded on every side by the yellow sea. Baloo watched from the fringe of the jungle, holding his breath.

But then the old bear faltered as he ran.

Baloo saw it. He saw one of the men turn, pause, his eyes narrowing, and then two more men hesitated in their flight. One began to lift his weapon.

Baloo didn't stop to think. He stepped out of the jungle, bounded down a few steps of the path, and gave the loudest roar of his life.

The men turned to stare. What they saw was a bear – but a bear flecked and striped in deep ochre yellow. A ball of black fur and teeth, patched in pieces of the sun.

Pita looked up and saw his son. Something in the sight gave a galvanic kick to the old bear's legs, and he began to speed, until he was running like a young cub, the pain in his paw forgotten, charging towards his boy.

But Baloo walked straight past him, back towards the village. He walked – did not run, but prowled, the only living creature moving forward against the tide of tiny animals heading in the opposite direction.

He hesitated, facing the three remaining men and their three guns, feverishly trying to think of the right words. Words, he knew, can win a battle.

"Stay away! We are not yours to take." He roared it in Bear, and then in Wolf and Tiger, and then in Mouse and Rat and Jerboa, vicious squeaks coming from his black muzzle.

Finally, he roared it in his best imitation of the Human tongue.

The men stared, stunned. They did not move. One man murmured a prayer. "It speaks," he breathed.

Baloo paused for breath. There was a moment of total silence. Then the men began to move, to stir themselves and shake their heads, as if they were dreaming.

A great jolt of adrenaline bounded through Baloo's blood. He turned and galloped as fast as his short legs could carry him, back towards the deep green safety of the jungle, back towards his father, who was waiting to bite him on the back of the neck and growl a rough and wild thank you into the ear of his clumsiest, slowest, bravest son.

'Everything changed after that day.

Or rather, not everything: some animals still thought Baloo was a foolish kind of bear – not to be trusted not to accidentally swing his vast bottom into your nose while you were eating.

But the jungle changed. The animals began to speak to one another. There were some very eccentric accents and some very bad grammar at first. But slowly, gradually, all the Peoples of the Jungle began to know one another's languages, as if it was the most natural thing in the world; as if it had always been that way.

There are days, perhaps, when Baloo will seem unnecessarily strict, when he roars at you if you haven't yet mastered how to say "Good day" in Monitor Lizard. But understand this: Baloo knows that words are life and death. Without Baloo, we would still be a jungle divided, blinking at one another silently in the sun and wishing we knew how to say, "We be of one blood, ye and I."'

Kaa's Dance

Mowgli rose to all fours and arched his spine thoughtfully. 'I still don't think he should have hit me,' he said. A fly landed on his rib and he flicked it away with his toe. 'But I like the part about the jerboas. I've always liked their ears.'

Akela growled in exasperation. He was on the cusp of repeating his speech about language and life and death when the trees around them began to shake. A howl tore through the air.

'That's your mother, surely?' said Akela. Reflexively his hackles rose, but his eyes were puzzled. 'What ails her?'

'Nothing!' said Mowgli.

'That noise doesn't suggest "nothing".'

'I meant . . . I'll go and find out.'

'Mowgli! Wait, she'll be here in just—'

Mowgli ducked his head as he ran, pell-mell, down the Council Rock, grateful for the thick covering to his feet and palms as he slipped and sped down the hot stone, grazing his skin against the jagged ridges in the surface.

As he tore past the waterhole, he stumbled over a cluster of rats. 'Your esteemed matriarch is desirous of your presence, young human child,' said the largest rat.

Mowgli blinked, standing on one leg.

A turtle lifted his head from the water. 'He means your mother wants to see you,' he said.

'I know,' said Mowgli grimly. 'But that doesn't mean *I* want to see *her.*'

He used the back of an unsuspecting buffalo as a springboard to jump into a rubber tree, and from there surveyed the vast knotted expanse ahead of him. The light beat down through the trees on to his skin, casting it a deep green. He could go either of two ways: towards the river, where he might be able to hide in the stream – wolves are not keen swimmers – or towards the Cold Lairs, where the snake Kaa slept.

Mowgli's appetite for stories had been whetted. He was hungry for more. He brushed a caterpillar off his eyebrow and went in search of Kaa, shinning up a vine until his head broke over the canopy.

Far above, the pair of red eyes blinked, satisfied. Four limbs stretched and creaked. Four paws began to make their way down the slope of the rock face.

Mowgli roamed the trees, chewing at a fig with one hand and climbing with the other, asking the smaller snakes for directions. When at last he found the great snake, Kaa was moving slowly along the branches of a tree flowering in white blooms, the petals falling on his vast back as he glided forward.

Mowgli transferred the fig to between his toes, grabbed a vine, and swung into the white tree, planning to land directly in front of the snake's eyes. He slightly misjudged it, and was about to topple on to the branch below, but the snake's tail came whipping round and steadied him. Mowgli hissed in thanks and sat down with his legs straddling the branch.

'Tell me a story, Kaa,' said Mowgli. He wiped fig juice off his chin.

'Why? And about what?'

'Just because. About anything.'

Kaa waited.

'If you would be so gracious,' said Mowgli, with a sigh.

Kaa flickered his tongue, laughing. 'I can think of only one subject that truly merits the telling,' he said. He wound himself into a vast coil in the crook of a tree.

'Then tell me that one!' Mowgli crossed over to him and clambered into the centre of the coil.

'Only *I* know this story – pray do not get fig juice on my skin – for only I have been alive long enough to remember it.'

'Good,' said Mowgli, and he set his cheek against the snake's cool smooth back, stretching out as if on a throne.

'By the time he was fully grown,' the snake began, 'Kaa was twenty-four feet long, which is the size of four tall humans lying with their feet on each other's heads.'

'Is this a story about *you*?' asked Mowgli, sitting up indignantly.

'Have you an objection?' said Kaa. And he flickered his tongue dangerously at the man-child.

'No!' said Mowgli quickly. 'None at all.' He picked his nose and ate the snot to show he was not afraid.

'By the time he was fully grown,' the snake repeated, 'Kaa was the longest and most magnificent of all the jungle snakes. But when he was young, he was small enough to fit in a basket. Kaa was a python—'

'I know *that*!' interrupted Mowgli. 'I don't need to be told that.'

'Hush!' hissed Kaa. 'I will tell it my way, or not at all.'

'Fine,' muttered Mowgli. He scratched at a spider bite on his chin and defiantly flicked the scab into Kaa's coils. 'Go on.'

'He was a python,' said Kaa again, 'a snake with elegant manners, shining coils and long teeth. And once, long ago, he belonged to a snake charmer who lived near the palace of Udaipur. Most snake charmers work in this way: they play an instrument called a pungi, and the snake rears up and seems – to idiots, at least – to dance. As if a snake would dance at a human's command!'

Mowgli nodded. He thought of Baloo's father, forced to walk on his hind legs. Humans seemed obsessed with making other creatures dance. 'What kind of instrument is it?' he asked.

'A gourd attached to two reeds that makes a sound when a Man blows into it – beautiful sounds, apparently, though I wouldn't know. Most snakes can't hear the music – we don't have the right kind of ear – but a snake's head will follow the movement of the pungi as it's played, ready to strike.'

'Why?' said Mowgli, laughing. 'There's nothing dangerous about a musical instrument!'

'Because the snakes have been taught to see the pungi as a threat,' said Kaa drily. 'In some cases they are beaten with it when they are very young.'

'But—'

'Don't interrupt. It looks as if the snake is dancing, but in fact, it is readying itself for battle. But the watching Men laugh and applaud; they think the snake is a foolish pet, no better than a dog who sits up to beg for scraps.'

'That's horrible!'

'There are some charmers who try to be kind; they don't understand how it wounds the vanity of the snake to be watched and laughed at. But there are others . . .' Kaa's face grew cold; even colder than usual. 'Some pull out the fangs of the snake. They put their bare fingers in the mouth of a viper – can you imagine the indignity! And the taste!'

Mowgli fingered his own teeth gingerly. 'But don't they grow back?'

'They do. A snake's fangs grow back within days, so the charmers plug the gap with wax. "Wax-mouth" is a terrible insult among snakes. And there are some charmers who do even worse.'

'How could they possibly do worse?'

'They – no, don't turn away, listen to me – they sew the snakes' mouths shut.'

Mowgli was wide-eyed. 'But what happens to them? How do they eat?'

'They don't. Those snakes invariably die.'

'That's terrible! That's disgusting and wrong!' Mowgli sat up and stared around, the hair along his back rising, as if looking for snake charmers to fight.

'It is. It is unforgivable. But then, too, there are the rare snake charmers who truly do understand the snake. Kaa knew one such once.'

'You mean, *you* once knew one,' said Mowgli. 'Why don't you say *I*?'

With spectacular dignity, Kaa ignored him. 'The charmer was unusual in three ways, for a snake charmer,' he said. 'Younger than most, and wilder and scrappier than most, and she was a girl-child. She lived in a small, sun-drenched house on the outskirts of the city with her great-aunt, and she caught the great python in a corner of the kitchen, back when he was barely three feet long. But—'

'Didn't you fight?'

'Of course I did! As I was just about to say – Kaa fought and bit and hissed, and soon the girl realized that she had found a snake of unusual strength and beauty, and with a ferociously unruly temper. But Kaa, back then, was not nearly as large as he is now, and there was something about the girl-child that made him reluctant to bite. So, at last, he allowed himself to be captured. Now stop interrupting.'

Mowgli laid his hand on the back of the snake's neck and felt the cool strength of his muscles. Kaa really was, he thought, amazingly beautiful. 'I won't any more.'

'Quite. Don't. The girl, whose name was Shivani, dusted him off and set him in a basket with loose-woven bars. She crouched, and stared at him, eye to eye.'

'*Then* did you bite her?'

Kaa glared at Mowgli. Mowgli ducked his head and grinned.

'No, Kaa did not bite. He stared back. The girl had a bump on the bridge of her nose and one unruly eyebrow. He had never met a human who was willing to meet his gaze. Usually they ran away screaming, the smallest ones with water spewing from their eyes. This one had a spark in her look that he liked. She seemed fearless. A smile began to twitch at the left corner of her mouth. An idea had flickered into life.

The next day, Shiv woke early. She lifted Kaa in his basket and crept with him into the kitchen, glancing behind her as she went, and lifted down a bowl from a high shelf.

The bowl was gold-coated and gloriously carved. Images of snakes twisted all around its base and lip, and the beaten metal transformed the daylight into a treasure trove. It shone. It had belonged to Shiv's great-great-grandmother, and it was worth more than everything else they owned put together. But even when there was no money in the house, and Shiv's feet had grown so that a whole inch of toe stuck out past the end of her sandals,

there was no question of selling it; it was their piece of something beautiful.

Shiv's great-aunt had told her, again and again, that Shiv was not allowed to touch it: never, not with the tip of her finger, not even if the house was falling down.

"Don't tell," Shiv whispered. "She'll never know. Or if she does, she'll understand." Even to Kaa, who was not versed in the tones of the human voice, the girl sounded unconvincing.

She stacked the bowl inside the basket, clutched them both to her ribcage, and tried to lift. Her muscles strained. Inside, Kaa gave a hiss that sounded even to human ears like a laugh.

"Fine, laugh!" she said. "But you *have* to be in a basket: that's how it works. If you went down the street in daylight by yourself, you'd cause a riot."

She went slowly down the steps to the street, accidentally bumping Kaa's basket against the wall.

"Sorry!" she said. "Nearly there."

A barefoot boy with a dimple in his chin looked round, startled, staring at the girl who was apparently apologizing to a basket.

Shiv made her way along narrow roads, dodging her great-aunt's friends down sweltering-hot back-streets, until she reached the steps in front of the outer walls of the City Palace. From inside the basket, Kaa heard – or rather felt vibrating along the earth – the quiet step of a bare foot following half a street behind.

Shiv, sweating with the effort, positioned the basket at the bottom of the steps. It stood in a sun-bright patch of pavement, where the occasional visitors passed by on their way to stare up at the palace walls.

Shiv sat down cross-legged behind it. She placed the gold bowl in front of the basket. She fished inside her clothes and drew out a very old, very battered pungi.

Kaa watched through the weave of the basket as the girl tried to rearrange the features of her face – squinting her eyes, sucking in her nostrils – to look older and more imposing. It was not, he thought, particularly impressive.

A small crowd gathered to stare at her. They murmured to one another that they had never seen a child snake charmer before. They murmured that the girl was *sweet*. Kaa wondered how they knew that; they had not, as far as he could see, bitten her.

Then Shiv began to play. Her playing was not in truth very good: she knew no tunes, only scales, and she played them up and down the length of the pungi. But it did not matter. Kaa was bored of the basket. He tensed his muscles and heaved himself up and out, over the wicker edge, swarming on to the warm roadside.

There was a scream. "He'll kill us all!" a man roared, beads of sweat forming on his top lip. "He's supposed to stay in the basket!"

Shiv held up her hands to the crowd. "Please don't panic – don't go! He's very gentle," she said.

Kaa whipped his head round to face the girl. He was *not* gentle, and did not like being called so. He let out a long, threatening hiss.

The reaction was gratifying. Several people shrieked. A small boy on his father's shoulders yelped and spat out his mouthful of banana on to the bald head of the man in front of him. The entire crowd shifted backwards in a human wave.

Kaa looked at the rows of terrified human eyes. Some deep

instinct inside his blood began to stir. A hunger rose up in him. Slowly he began to twist across the earth floor, casting shapes like a shadow across the moon. He felt his audience tense, felt them sway on the balls of their feet. He moved faster and faster, casting dust across the watchers' shoes.

The crowd began to grow very still. Nobody laughed or shouted. Nobody rustled or coughed.

There was something unusual about their stillness. Kaa had never seen a crowd of men so motionless. A human, he knew, is always eating its own fingernails, or inserting some portion of its hand inside its nose . . .'

Kaa paused to look pointedly at Mowgli. Mowgli hurriedly took his finger out of his left nostril and wiped it on his hair.

'The snake,' Kaa continued, 'gave a flick of his tail, towards the Royal Gate.'

'The great mass of people leaned a little towards the great portico.

Kaa hissed in pleasure. He backed away half an inch. Every human moved half an inch closer.

Shiv was still playing, but her eyes were as round and panicked as a buck before the kill, and she shook her head at Kaa.

Kaa surged forward. The crowd fell back, but not as if afraid: more as if it were some great sixty-legged creature, moving to the young snake's command. Kaa swung his neck and head to the left. The crowd stepped left.

Kaa felt delight surge through his scales. He danced faster now, twisting his head left and right, high and low, and the crowd mirrored his movements like a reflection in a river.

Kaa ended his dance. The crowd stood, rock-still, tree-still, sun-still. Then, slowly, they seemed to shake off the influence. A man blinked; a woman scratched her head.

Shiv got to her feet. "This is the part where you pay me," she called. She held out the bowl.

The crowd ignored her. They turned to go, some laughing,

some confused. A few were glaring around them, as if someone had tricked them into doing something embarrassing.

"Right," said Shiv. She bent, heaved Kaa over her shoulders like a scarf, picked up the bowl, and began to approach the onlookers. She had a determinedly aggressive smile on her face. Kaa smiled at them too, his tongue flickering; then they hurriedly reached into their second skins and produced money.

❧

Shiv resisted counting it until they reached the safety of her home. Kaa swarmed up the window frame and hung himself comfortably from the top of it. Shiv had just poured the coins on to the table when the latch of the door clicked. She gasped, darted across the room, and balanced the gold bowl on the shelf. It was still gently vibrating when her great-aunt walked into the room; but humans, Kaa had noted, do not notice vibrations, or indeed anything at all, unless they are very unusual specimens.

The great-aunt stared at the pile of coins on the table. "Shiv!" she said. "What's this?"

Shiv grinned up at her; but her great-aunt did not smile back.

"Oh, Shiv," she said, "what have you done?"

"What do you mean?" Every line on Shiv's face fell downward. Watching her, Kaa felt a surprisingly strong desire to bite the great-aunt.

"Did you steal it? We're not rich, Shiv, but we're not desperate—"

"Of course I didn't!" said Shiv. "I'd never steal! I've been working in the market – just by the City Palace."

"Doing what?"

Kaa saw Shiv hesitate, dip her eyes, before she told an outright lie. "Just carrying bags and things."

Now, snakes do not have much in the way of a moral code. There are a few laws, handed down for thousands of years: Thou shalt not hunt thy own species. Thou shalt not tell the secrets of another. And Thou shalt not lie.

This last is a practicality: a python believes that lying is a hot-blooded trick, far beneath its dignity; and besides, pythons live so long that every single one of its lies would be discovered. Kaa hissed disapprovingly and felt Shiv's cheeks grow hot. Still, he thought, she was only a human. And she had guts, and flair, and unusual eyes.

Every day that next week, Shiv took Kaa to the pavement outside the City Palace. Sometimes, she took a cloth hat that had once belonged to her grandfather for the people to throw money in. Sometimes, when she dared, she fetched down the gold bowl from where it stood in splendour on the shelf.

When Shiv passed the bowl around instead of the hat, they got almost twice the money. People wanted to hear the great metallic bowl ring to the sound of the falling coins.

The fame of Kaa and Shiv began to spread, and the crowds to grow thick. Kaa rather looked forward to his dance; there was a heady pleasure in seeing the crowd move to his command. Not even the Maharana, Kaa told himself, had that power. A niggle in his young brain told him it was beneath him to dance for human coins in the dust of the street, but Shiv's eyes and hair had shone brighter since there was money for milk and tomatoes and sweet jalebi, and although Kaa knew that snakes did not and could not love humans, there was pleasure in seeing her grow glossy.

Then, two full weeks after Kaa's first dance, just as Shiv sat down outside the palace gates and Kaa rose up to dance, everything went wrong.

The crowd had just begun to sway when a shout came down the street. A boy came hurtling around a corner, dust flying up behind him, running barefoot over the hot stone pavement.

A guardsman came skidding down the street, roaring in rage: "Stop him! Catch him!"

The boy darted into the middle of the crowd, fast followed by the guardsman.

Kaa's tongue flickered. He could taste fear in the air, and hunger – the boy's hunger – though it was not a hunger for food.

The guardsman's eyes scanned the crowd; he looked at Shiv, at Kaa. Kaa could see the boy: he was crouched on his haunches, right in the middle of the crowd.

He was barefoot, and he had a deep dimple in his chin. But the guardsman's eyes, like all human eyes, were weak, and he stared wildly around.

"Where is he?" he asked. "You're hiding him!"

Shiv jumped to her feet and backed against the wall. "I don't know! I've never seen him before!"

"It's a trick!" said the guardsman. Then he bent and snatched up the golden bowl. He clutched it to his chest. "If you won't cooperate, I'm taking this. This is money unlawfully got," he said. He stared again into the crowd. "I'm confiscating it."

"Give that back!" said Shiv. "Snake charming isn't illegal!"

"Thieving is," said the guard. "You and that boy are working together."

Kaa decided he did not like the man's tone. He surged towards the guardsman, who hit out wildly with his baton; Kaa reared his head back, readied his muscles, and struck his fangs into the man's arm as it swooped downward. It was a peculiar taste – sharp and thin – and not attractive. He made a note never to eat a man if he could help it.

The guardsman gave a roar, louder than any Kaa had heard, and tried to stamp on him with his black boots.

Kaa heaved himself forward into the crowd, weaving in and out among people's feet. It had the desired effect. The trance broke; he could almost feel it shattering. He hissed again, and everyone, including the guardsman, scattered before him. Shiv was left breathless, alone on the street, wide-eyed, her hair falling over her face. She hefted Kaa around her neck and began sprinting home.

Two streets away from her house, a voice called out.

"Hey!" it said. "You forgot this!"

The barefoot boy stood in front of Shiv, holding out Kaa's wicker basket, a wide smile on his face. Shiv took it without speaking.

"Aren't you going to say thank you?" asked the boy.

"No," said Shiv.

"Well, you should! Where are your manners?" He grinned again, a slightly less confident grin this time. "I'm Arjun, by the way."

Shiv stared at him. Kaa could see the muscles working in her jaw. "You should get away from me before I yell for the police."

"Look, I'm sorry about your bowl, but I didn't know what that guard was going to do, did I? Did you want me to get arrested?"

"You could have hidden somewhere else!"

"There wasn't anywhere else! Nowhere as good, anyway. And I never get caught. I thought it would be fine!"

"Well, it's not fine, all right? It's absolutely, utterly *not fine*. That man has my great-aunt's most treasured thing! She'll kill me. She'll *hate* me." Shiv took in a breath that shook her body and thrummed along Kaa's spine. "And . . . she'll know what I've been doing, that I knew she was worried about money. She'll be so ashamed."

Arjun didn't miss a beat; the smile on his face faltered only for a second. "We'll get it back!"

"*How*? How are we possibly going to get it back? He's one of the palace guards." Shiv let out the beginnings of a wail, but she bit it back. She scrubbed away a tear from the corner of her eye. Kaa watched as she forced herself to straighten her spine.

Kaa felt something flicker in his heart, something like pride, as he felt her draw herself upward. He did not, of course, love her, for she was only a human, but still he wound himself a little tighter around her neck.

Kaa saw Shiv's fingers twitch. Not an idea, but the beginnings of one. "Where will he have taken the bowl?"

"To the guardhouse, probably – the one just outside the east gate of the palace. That's where he works."

"And you're a thief, aren't you? A pickpocket?"

He glared. "A street artist."

"You're a thief. Can you also pick locks?"

"Yes, if I want."

"And could you pick the lock on the guardhouse door?"

"Of course I could, if I had time. I'd need a distraction. The whole key to street-work is misdirection."

"What?"

"Misdirection. When you make someone look the wrong way. Look, I'll show you!" Arjun stepped to stand directly in front of Shiv. "Watch – if I move my hand like this, in an arc –" Arjun traced a rainbow shape across the air – "your eye follows my hand, and when it stops moving, your eye stays on the hand. But if I move my hand in a straight line, horizontally – see, like this – your eye snaps back to the starting place. It's all about where people look. I'd need some misdirection."

"That's fine," said Shiv, and she raised her hand to Kaa's back. "He could misdirect an entire army."

"So what's the plan?"

Shiv pulled Arjun closer, to whisper. "Petitioners are allowed to come to the guardhouse to ask to perform for the Royal Family, right? Dancers and jugglers and things."

"Yes! But they almost never get let in."

"So we'll say, 'Watch us here first, and then tell the Maharana how good we are.' And then Kaa will dance, and you'll break into the guardhouse."

"The guardsman won't let us do any kind of show! He knows us! He'll just kick us out immediately!"

"Only if he recognizes us. We'll dress differently, in gold, or something. And we'll say I'm the most famous snake charmer in Madhya Pradesh."

Arjun shook his head. "No. It's just too risky. Breaking in with him right there? We'll both be caught!"

Shiv bit her lip, hard enough to draw blood. "I know. But we have to try. I can't force you to help – but if you've got any courage at all, you'll be at my door tomorrow at dawn." And she slipped down a side street and away.

As Kaa rode home, draped around Shiv's neck, he thought about the plan. It was true, probably, that he could hypnotize an army. He could hypnotize most things: people, cats, monkeys, birds. The only true hypnotists, he knew, were snakes. Hypnosis among Men is almost always a trick: a person planted in a crowd beforehand, or a person so eager to believe that they get dizzy and call it a trance. But a snake's hypnosis is as real as blood and bone.

Kaa was beginning to discover that he was good at it. Indeed, Kaa was beginning to believe that he might, at only a few years old, be a master. He could rearrange the mind of the wisest old

woman in Seoni. He could make people sleep while they woke.

Shiv stroked him and ran the tip of his tail through her fingers. She didn't know that she had the most talented hypnotist the world had ever known wrapped around her neck.

Shiv's great-aunt had not noticed the missing bowl. Every time she glanced at the wall, Shiv's heart swooped down to her knees, but the old woman's eyesight wasn't what it had been, and Shiv went to bed full of hope that the plan might actually work.

Her confidence, though, seemed to evaporate in the night. At sunrise, she climbed out of bed and stood looking out of the kitchen door; her forehead was creased and wrinkled with worry, marked like the bark of an ancient tree.

"It's not going to work," she said. "What if Arjun doesn't come?"

Kaa flickered his tongue. He agreed with her. It almost certainly wouldn't.

"And even if he does, the guard will recognize me!"

Kaa waited, twitching his tail to chase a fly off Shiv's foot.

"Even if I cover my face with my hair, there can't be that many girl snake charmers; he'll know it's me." She stared at Kaa. Then, slowly (very slowly indeed: humans are not fast thinkers), he could see a fresh idea come to her.

"What if I didn't dress as a girl? What if I was a *boy* snake charmer?" A vast half-moon smile broke across her face. "What if I borrow Arjun's clothes?"

Kaa writhed across the floor, tracing celebratory shapes. But then Shiv's face began to fall again. "But what about you? What if he recognizes you? You're the most beautiful snake in the world; he must have noticed what you look like."

Kaa did not disagree. He was indeed the most beautiful snake in the world, and he did not believe that modesty was a virtue.

"I know!" Shiv let out a sudden shout of triumph. "We could paint you."

Kaa tried to convey, as best he could, that they absolutely could not. He opened his jaws wide and showed his teeth.

"I know, I know!" Shiv knelt down in front of Kaa, stroked his back. "But it's so urgent."

Kaa considered. It was a grotesque idea, of course. But the girl was in his care. She was under his protection. He hadn't asked for the responsibility, but it had come, gradually, like the night: she was his.

"I won't use real paint! I'll use something that comes off easily."

Kaa sighed. He surged up Shiv's arm and looped himself round her neck.

Shiv ran to the store cupboard, pulled out a pestle and mortar and began to crush dried seeds and spices, then added water. "Look! Chili. See? Like paint – but it tastes better." She dabbed a taste of it on the snake's nose. He jerked away, hissing; some of it transferred to the roof of his mouth, where it burned hideously, and Kaa writhed away into a corner of the kitchen.

"Sorry!" she said. Very slowly, she approached him with one coated finger. "You don't need to taste it. And look – it will wash off!"

Shiv had just finished painting Kaa's back with bright red stripes when there was a knock on the kitchen door. Before she could reach it, the lock clicked, and it swung open.

Arjun crouched on the ground outside, a length of wire in his hand and a huge grin on his face.

"Told you I could pick locks," he said. He had a long gold cloth over one arm.

"You came!" said Shiv.

Arjun wiped his nose with the back of his hand, elaborately casual. "Had to, didn't I? Look! This belongs to my second cousin; it's a curtain, but you should be able to make it into a dress."

"Perfect!" said Shiv. She did not look up from where she was crouched over Kaa's back, painting. "Except I've decided I'm going to wear trousers instead."

"Whose?"

"Yours."

"But then what will I wear?"

Shiv grinned. "I'm sure we'll think of something."

It was a peculiar band that approached the guardhouse.

A boy led the party. He wore a hat, scruffy trousers and a shirt that smelt strongly of running and hiding, and his eyes were full of determination. Behind him, a taller boy came slouching, clad in a toga made from a length of gold curtain. He kicked up the dust ahead of him as he went.

Around the smaller boy's neck there was a snake. The snake was striped brown and vivid scarlet, and its eyes flashed redder than the most highly polished ruby.

A tail of small children began to follow them as they walked through the narrow streets, laundry hanging overhead. Kaa smiled at the smallest of the man-cubs; they screamed and scattered, giggling, then returned at a safer distance.

The guardhouse stood just outside the west gates, in the shadow of the palace. The house walls were bright white and dazzlingly clean. Two cats, one white and one tabby, waited by the door for scraps.

Shiv's steps began to slow as they came nearer. Kaa could feel her muscles shaking under her clothes. He let his tongue dart out and touch the back of her hand; the flicker of the tongue said, *You're safe. You're with me.*

Shiv felt it and seemed to understand. She pulled back her shoulders and raised her chin. She knocked on the door. The guard looked out, still chewing something. Shiv's stomach swooped at the sight of him. "What do you want?" he asked.

A mange-ridden black cat prowled up, attracted by the spark of Arjun's golden drapings. It was followed by a ginger kitten. Arjun reached down to stroke it, hiding his face from the guard.

"We are a travelling troupe from the other side of Madhya Pradesh," said Shiv. Her voice wobbled. "We wish to perform before the Maharana."

The guard laughed. "A troupe of two? Get lost, kids."

"No, wait!" Shiv held up her hand, and Kaa hissed. "You have to watch us. Really! We're the best there's ever been."

Without waiting for a yes or a no, she sat down in the dust in front of the door and pulled out her pungi.

As she put it to her lips, she peered through the window into the gloom of the guard's hut. There on a high shelf was her bowl, catching the light and turning it a brighter shade of gold. She blew an unnecessarily loud note as she saw it, and Kaa felt it thrum through him. He reared up and began to dance.

It was the greatest dance of his life. He traced loops and figure of eights with his body, and fast, wild triangles that melted into squares, and five-sided figures, and coiled mounds, and all the while he hissed a sharp song that cut at the air.

The effect was immediate. The children who had clustered round took a step backwards, and then their shoulders and necks and elbows and knees seemed to become loose and supple. They began to sway in time. The eyes of the adults grew wide, and their mouths fell open. The crowd began to rock backwards and forwards together. Kaa hissed with pleasure. He jerked his neck, and the crowd stepped closer: closer to Shiv, closer to Arjun, closer to the door of the guardhouse.

The guard watched. At first he seemed only annoyed, but swiftly Kaa's magic began to work on him. His eyes started to look dreamy, as if he were remembering something complicated and beautiful and long ago.

Arjun caught Shiv's eye and nodded. He turned away from the crowd and knelt in front of the keyhole to the door with a length of wire in his hand. Kaa's eyes darted around the square, looking for any stray passer-by who had not yet fallen under his spell. But the whole mass of humanity around him seemed to be safely bewitched.

And then the plan began to fall apart.

Kaa gave an unusually vigorous twist to his body, and his tail caught a loose rock in the paving and flicked it, skittering, across the square to land at the guard's feet.

The guard jerked and stirred; his eyebrows worked up and down like angry toothbrushes. He was fighting Kaa's spell. He let out a noise that was somewhere between a groan and a burp.

There were only seconds to act. Kaa took his eyes off the crowd and turned his attention to the cats.

Cats are harder to hypnotize than humans. They have too much self-respect to like the idea of giving up control of their own brains. But Kaa worked harder than he ever had in his life, sending his whole body swirling across the stone floor, even as his head and eyes were stock-still, staring into each cat's eyes.

Three more tomcats appeared, as if answering a call. Their tails began to swish backwards and forwards in time to Shiv's music.

Arjun wiped sweaty hands on his curtain. The lock gave a click. He pushed at the door. It didn't open.

The cats stopped twitching their tails. They grew deadly still.

Kaa jerked his head backwards. The cats stepped forward, towards Kaa.

The guard let out another noise: a muttering, angry sound, the gurgle of a furious thought trying to surface.

Arjun pushed again at the door. Sweat dripped on to the stone floor. The door would not open.

Then several things happened at once. The guard turned his head, very slowly, to stare at Arjun. A dream-slow "*Hey!*" formed on his lips. Shiv sprinted to Arjun, put her shoulder next to his, and gave the door a hard shove.

And Kaa gave a great swirl to his body and woke the fury in the cats.

A cat's fury is a terrifying thing: a red-hot, fever-eyed rage; a fury so electric, it makes the air crackle. The cats launched themselves into the air and straight at the guard.

Shiv shrieked. The first cat's front claws went straight for the guard's face, its hind legs gouging at his shoulders.

There were cats on his head, on his back, biting at his neck, scratching at his eyes and clawing at the insides of both his nostrils.

The door burst open. Arjun stood guard while Shiv darted inside and seized the bowl.

"Run!" he called. "Now, quick, before they all wake up and stop us!"

Shiv grabbed Kaa and swung him around her neck. Arjun grabbed her free hand, and together they ran as they had never run in their lives before, out of the square and down the side alleys, leaving a crowd of gently swaying men and women and the cries of a single, furious, cat-covered guard.

Shiv waited until it was entirely dark before she crept out of the house that night. She lifted Kaa from his place above her door frame and carried him in her arms to the kitchen. They stopped in front of the golden bowl as it stood, shining in the moonlight, in the middle of the shelf. Kaa, however, was looking not at the bowl, but at Shiv. He flickered his tongue against the soft skin between her thumb and forefinger. He had a sense already of what it was that Shiv planned to do.

She pulled on shoes, trying to be silent – though the most silent human is as loud as a herd of elephants, compared to a snake – and crept out into the dark.

The dark closed around them as Shiv walked down the winding street, but she was not afraid. For now, at least, she had the best protection possible: a python as long as she was tall, and as brave as the world entire.

❧

An hour out of the city, the roads gave way to open country. Shiv stopped. There, in the distance, was the great green smudge of the jungle.

"I can't keep you," Shiv said. "The guard would come for you. We'll be all right, me and Auntie and Arjun – but it's not safe for you."

Her voice, which had been steady, wavered suddenly, and a single drop of water fell on Kaa's head.

"Besides," she said, "you're getting too big to live in a house. You need space to grow. You're going to be the biggest and most beautiful snake in the world."

And before Kaa could do more than flicker his tongue one last time against her palm, she had laid him down on the dirt path and turned back the way she had come.

Kaa did not go immediately to the jungle that night. The girl, he thought, was far too young and thin-boned to be walking alone in the dark. He slid into the long black speargrass by the wayside and followed her, unseen, back to the house: a secret bodyguard. He saw her lock the door behind her, safe.

Then he turned and headed back the way he had come, faster than any human pace, back to the jungle that was waiting to become his home.

It would have been absolutely wrong to say that Kaa loved the girl. He could not, even if he had wanted to: Kaa was a python, and snakes are many ranks above humans. But she was an unusual human, and Kaa was an unusual python. So.'

Kaa paused and looked hard at Mowgli. He unwound and rewound himself around the branch, unusually restless for a snake.

'That was a long time ago,' he said. 'Shiv will have grown old, and grown wrinkled, and died. I never saw her again. But I do think – just very occasionally – about what her children, grandchildren and great-grandchildren would have been like.' He looked at Mowgli's nose, which had a bump in it, just below his unruly eyebrows. 'I think they would have been unusual too.'

Mowgli

Mowgli knelt up on Kaa's coils and began sharpening his stone knife on the sole of his foot. He grinned at Kaa. 'I can't repay you in tales, but I can drive a buck into your jaws. Will you hunt with me?'

Kaa shook his great head. 'I ate some days ago.' He yawned, opening his jaws so wide that he almost swallowed his own face. 'I'm tired. I'll lie here a little longer. Come back next week.'

Mowgli bent his head in salute to the old snake, and tucked his knife into the cloth he wore around his waist.

'Good hunting,' said Kaa. 'And stay safe, little frog. There's a tension in the air these last past hours. There's a smell in the air that says nothing good.'

Mowgli laughed. 'I'll be fine!' He grasped the branch of the tree in one hand and hauled himself up into the leaves. 'Stay well, old dancer!' he called down, and took off at a run along the thick branches over the snake's head.

It was almost dark when he got back to the wolf cave. His brother was chewing on the back leg of a buck. He leaped to all four paws as Mowgli approached.

'Mowgli! Where have you been all day? Mother's been searching the whole jungle.'

'I've been here and there.' Mowgli grinned. 'Collecting things.'

'What? Food?'

'Not exactly. Tales.'

'Oh. What good's that?'

Mowgli shrugged. 'It's hard to say, for now. One day they might be useful.'

He was just bending to tear a mouthful of meat from Brother Wolf's kill when Raksha came bounding up the slope towards them.

'You're here!' She dipped her nose to Mowgli's, her breath ragged against his.

Mowgli's whole body became tense. She did not look angry; she looked panicked. There was sweat in her fur. The air around her tasted of some strong emotion.

He jumped to his feet. 'Something's wrong,' he said. 'It's not the eagle-owl's nest, is it?'

'What owl?' Mother Wolf was still panting, barely able to talk, her tongue lolling from her mouth.

'What is it?'

Mother Wolf swallowed. 'He's come!'

'Who?' Mowgli dropped to all fours. He flexed his knees, ready to fight.

'He's come down. From the mountain. The ape.'

'What ape?'

'The ancient white ape!' Raksha stared at her son. 'Three times the size of a man-child. Did the elephants never tell you?'

'I thought that was just a story! Like the spirit of the wild dogs in the wind!'

Raksha let out a low growl: fear, not anger. 'You will wish that it were. Shere Khan woke him.'

'Why? Why would Shere Khan do so jungle-fevered a thing? Is he unhinged?'

'Shere Khan likes chaos. He likes discord. Where there is fighting, there is meat. And if the white ape has stalked down the mountain, he won't return until he has what he came for, even if it means lavish killing.'

'What did he come for?'

'We're not yet sure. The kites are trying to spy as best they can. But I fear I can guess; they say he wants an heir.'

Mowgli didn't know the word. 'An heir?'

'A family – someone to take his place when he dies.'

'Then he can take one of the Bandar-log – the monkey people – and go! Surely a monkey will want a monkey.'

'No. The monkeys are loose-jawed, slack-brained things. He wants something with power.'

'A wolf?' Mowgli's heart dropped. He darted to the mouth of the cave and looked in at the youngest litter of wolf cubs, counting feverishly, but they were all still there.

'No,' said Raksha. 'We're too rough, too snappish. I fear he wants you.'

'Me?' Mowgli touched the knife at his hip. He felt his fingertips prickle. 'If he wants me, let him come.'

'No!' Raksha batted him backwards with one swing of her muzzle, sending him tumbling back towards the cave. 'Why do you think I have been searching for you all day? I didn't save you from the tiger all those years ago to lose you to an ape. You need to hide!'

Mowgli got to his feet, brushing the dust from his hair. 'Mother, I can't.'

'I knew you would say that! I tell you that you *can*, and you must. This is not your battle.'

'Even if I did hide – what then? Would you want me to wait while he tore apart nests and lairs looking for me? Would you want me to hide forever?'

Raksha bit a mouthful of Mowgli's hair, as she had done when he was young, and tugged it to make him listen. 'If he hurts others, we shall retaliate. If he needs killing, I will kill him.'

Mowgli looked at his mother. She was as lean and sharp-toothed as ever, but she was no longer as young as she once had been; he knew how her hind legs ached in the rains. Before he could answer, Father Wolf came charging through the bushes towards the cave mouth, scattering dragonflies.

'Where is he?' he rasped. 'Where is my human son?'

'I'm here! I'm unhurt. What have you heard?'

'There's a commotion down by the lichen rock. I'm not sure what; I heard it from the doves, and I never could understand their accent.'

'The lichen rock?'

'Yes – wait, Mowgli!'

But Mowgli had gone, running with his heels barely touching the ground, his thick soles landing on thorns and stones without registering a flicker of pain. He had grown recently, and his muscles felt like whips under his skin. He catapulted through the jungle as if released from a spring. Mother Wolf, born the fastest of the wolves, could barely keep up with him.

They arrived at the foot of the rock together, Mother Wolf heaving for breath, her tongue hanging almost to the ground, and Mowgli trying not to look winded at all.

Bagheera was already there. His face was cold; it looked like fury, but it was more than that: misery, and fear too, of the killing that might come.

'We're too late,' he said curtly. 'He swung down here with a gang of Bandar-log and has taken a cub.'

'A cub? Whose?'

'Putri and Putra, twin tiger cubs, barely three weeks old.'

'*Tigers?*' said Mowgli.

'Yes. A nephew and niece of Shere Khan's.'

'Shere Khan? But Shere Khan woke the ape in the first place!'

'I know,' said Bagheera. 'But I fear there is a logic to it.'

Mother Wolf stared at Bagheera incredulously. 'I thought he would want Mowgli! I thought that was why he had come down the mountain.'

'We can't just leave them there!' said Mowgli. 'We need to fetch them back!'

Raksha's eyes met Bagheera's. 'That is the logic, isn't it?' she said. 'The ape knew what my boy would say.'

'I believe he did, yes.'

Raksha turned to Mowgli, her teeth showing in a grimace. 'I won't let you risk your life for a couple of tiger cubs. Tigers are not our allies—'

'Not all tigers are the same!' interrupted Mowgli. 'Bagheera always says that! He says, *To live is to be wild and various.*'

'And I say again: it is not your battle!'

'It *is*, Mama! Any jungle battle is a battle of mine. Like you with Bhedi: you protect what you love.'

Raksha had opened her mouth to snap at him, but then she

stopped and sighed, a sigh so deep her whole body shook. She bowed her head. 'I don't like it,' she said. 'But I won't stop you.'

'Good!' Mowgli felt his body shiver with purpose. 'How do I get them back?' he asked.

'Not *I* but *we*, little frog,' said a voice. It came from behind him. Baloo came lumbering up, slow-footed and cumbersome, out of breath and puffing tiny balls of fur as he coughed. 'Is it true? The white ape has come?'

'It's true,' said Bagheera. His voice was very low.

'Then this will be an ugly day for all of us.'

Bagheera lifted his head. 'Listen.'

The wind stilled at that moment and, from far above their heads, near the top of the sheer face of rock, so faint it could almost be the wind, they could hear the unmistakable mew of a panicked tiger cub.

'Can you climb up there, little frog?' asked Baloo. He rocked back on his haunches and stared up the cliff. 'For I am certain none of us can.'

'Of course I can!' said Mowgli. 'Just watch!' He ran to the wall of rock and felt for a handhold. It was a sheer face of shining grey stone, spotted here and there with yellow lichen. He dug his fingers into a crevice and pulled himself up. 'Easy!'

He reached across for another handhold, and then for another. His fingers quaked with the effort.

Then, ten feet up the rock, he stopped abruptly. 'There's no place to grip,' he called down. 'I can't suction myself on like a lizard. And the lichen isn't strong enough to be a handhold.'

'Then come down!' called Raksha. 'Quick, there's no time to waste!'

Glaring at the rock face, Mowgli began to inch his way down again. He landed with a thump – a thump that sounded to him of humiliation.

'I can't get up there,' he said.

'Nobody could except the monkey people and the birds,' said Baloo. 'What are we to do? Do we leave the cubs up there to die?'

'Wait! The birds!' cried Mowgli. 'That story! The birds who lifted the buffalo skull for – for—' And he stopped suddenly at the look on Bagheera's face.

It felt as if the wind had been knocked out of him. Mowgli looked at the floor. There was a long pause.

Then: 'Go on,' said Bagheera.

Mowgli spoke quietly, stepping carefully into each of his words. 'I mean,' he said, 'the birds have helped before. They might help us again.'

'How? They aren't going to attack the ape themselves,' said Baloo. 'The great white ape holds the dread of myth to them; you do not try to bite or claw a myth.'

'Yes!' said Mowgli. 'But if they could lift a skull, they could lift me!'

'You weigh far more than a skull, little frog,' said Bagheera. 'You're not a cub any longer. The birds could never lift you in their claws. Apart from anything else, their talons would go straight through your skin to the bone.'

'Then we'll find another way! But we need to ask them to come! Not just the vultures – all the large birds – the eagles and the kites and even the pigeons!' He laid an urgent hand on

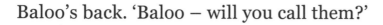

Baloo's back. 'Baloo – will you call them?'

Baloo growled at Mowgli. 'Have you not learned the calls yourself? Did I not tell you they would be needed one day?'

'I can do Kite,' said Mowgli, 'and Eagle. I'm not sure about Pigeon. It always seemed awkward, since I eat them. You don't.'

'Call for the kites and eagles,' said Baloo. 'And I will do the rest.'

Mowgli leaped into the branches of a tree and skittered feverishly to the top, to get as close as possible to the sky. His hands were sweating, not with fear, but with pure distilled urgency, and he could feel his heart smacking against his ribs.

'We be of one blood, you and I!' Mowgli called in Kite. And then, in Eagle, 'We be of one blood! Come! Come to the lichen rock! Spread the word! We have need of you!'

Baloo's call was more complicated. He called in Pigeon and Macaw and Raven, and in every call he was able to say more sophisticated – and politer – things. Finally, he called in Vulture. 'Come, strongest birds of all! Come, Vultures! The jungle has need of you!'

Mother Wolf and Bagheera crouched, watching. They did not join in. Wolves are not good at bird calls, and Bagheera never raised his voice.

The birds came slowly at first, in ones and twos; and then, as the message spread, the sky began to be dotted with them, flapping from across the whole great sweep of the jungle.

Mowgli ran to the nearest tree, his heart thumping in his chest. He gripped a handful of vines that hung down over his head and pulled them to the ground. 'Quick!' he called to Bagheera and Raksha. 'Help me bring these down. I'll need dozens – maybe a hundred.'

Quaking with concentration, his tongue between his teeth, he began to wind the vines into ropes, each three vines thick and fifteen feet long.

'What are you doing, little frog?' asked Bagheera, his mouth full of vines.

'I am making a flying machine,' said Mowgli.

'Mowgli, is this really the time for playing at inventions?' asked Raksha.

But Mowgli kept plaiting, his fingers working in a blur. Then, very carefully, he began to wind the vines around his waist and thighs, leaving each of the ropes with at least ten feet of vine still free. Then he looped more vines around his waist, tying them round and round each other until he appeared to be wearing a pair of thick green shorts attached to three dozen ropes. Kite watched, a sceptical tilt to his beak.

'There!' Mowgli bounded to his feet. 'See! The birds take the vines in their claws and fly upward – and I fly with them!'

Kite looked at the vines, at the cliff, at Mowgli. 'Absolutely not,' he said. 'Never in a thousand ages. No.'

The vultures hunched their wings so high above their heads in their disgust that they seemed at risk of dislocating their bones.

'Not today, not ever,' said one. 'We do not carry man-cubs about as if we were their servants.'

'Please!' said Mowgli. 'There are two tiger cubs at the top of the mountain.'

'And we need to get them down,' said Mother Wolf, 'before the ape grows tired of them and tosses them over the edge to be eaten by v—' She hesitated, balking at the word as she remembered who she was talking to.

The vulture shrugged. 'I wouldn't necessarily object to eating a dead tiger cub,' he said.

'Which won't be on the menu if we help,' said another.

'So you see the difficulty,' said a third.

Bagheera prowled forward. 'You did me a service once before,' he said to the vultures, 'and you found that I repaid my debt. Help the man-cub now, and I will lay out half my kill until the moon waxes and wanes three times. That is a more than fair exchange.'

The vultures looked at one another. The kites looked at one another. The pigeons looked, variously, at the sky, at a small heap of mouse droppings, and at an unusually shaped rock. They are an obliging if not particularly intelligent species of bird, and did not need any persuading: they were happy to do whatever Baloo asked them. At last the vultures nodded.

'Fine,' said Kite. 'We have a pact.'

'Quickly, then,' said Baloo. 'Each bird must wind a vine in his talons. It's important that you all take off at once. I'll count to three. One . . .'

'And remember,' added Raksha, 'if you drop him, there will be every wolf in the jungle to answer to.'

'Two . . .'

'Hold tight!' said Raksha to Mowgli.

'Three!'

The birds took off in a great cacophony of wings. Mowgli felt himself jerked off the ground, swung sideways, and spun wildly to the left. The rock face swung towards him, and he smacked against it with his shoulder, scraping away the skin.

'Back!' he cried. 'Back a little!'

He grabbed handfuls of vines and hauled himself to sit upright in his vine sling, brushing stray feathers from his eyes. The pigeons had to flap three times for each great beat of the eagles' wings, and so it was not a comfortable flight, but Mowgli felt himself swung higher and higher, until the animals below him were just a patch of grey, of brown, of black against the green. His stomach swooped drunkenly as he looked down. He bit his lip hard and looked upward instead.

They were coming in sight of a peak on the rock face; a crop in the stone came into view. Behind the shelf of rock there was a cave, and from inside the cave there was the sound of weeping.

'Let me down here!' called Mowgli. There was no point in trying to be quiet; the clatter of the birds' wings was loud enough to summon all but the deafest of creatures. Mowgli hoped very hard that the ape was indeed deaf.

The birds, squawking instructions to one another, lowered him as close to the shelf of rock as they could get, then, at a call from Kite, dropped him.

The vultures let go a second too late, and Mowgli was swung outward as he fell. He dropped three feet and landed with his ribs and elbows on the rock shelf, his legs swinging over thin air.

He gasped out a rude word in Lizard, scrambling desperately with his nails for purchase on the stone. A thorn tree grew from a gap in the rock; he grasped it, wincing at the spikes, and pulled.

His body inched forward. Grunting with effort, he swung his legs up and over on to the ledge and pulled himself to his feet. He was scraped and his knees were bleeding, but his bones felt intact.

He was just gathering the vines the birds had dropped and was winding them in a coil around his shoulder when there was a disturbance in the mouth of the cave. A voice emerged.

'Who is there?' It was a voice that sounded of dry-picked bones and a hundred winters. 'Show yourself! Come into the cave. I cannot see in the light.'

Mowgli edged forward. 'I am Mowgli. The man-cub.'

'So you came!' A shadow moved forward in the gloom. 'You're smaller than I imagined. You look like a scrap of dust – no more to you than a whisper.'

A pair of eyes appeared in the darkness of the cave. Mowgli swallowed. The eyes were shrewd and calculating, and they were as red as the heart of a fire.

'Well, I'm not a whisper,' said Mowgli. 'I'm blood and bone. And teeth.' He rolled back his lips, as his mother had taught him.

Just then the two cubs came skittering into the light out of the cave, keening in fear. They were barely old enough to know how their paws worked, and they kept slipping on the rock. Mowgli was afraid they would skid straight over the edge and into nothingness. He reached forward to pick them up.

'Don't touch them!' snapped the ape. 'Or I'll sweep them off the edge of the cliff and you with them.'

Mowgli froze.

'Come closer,' said the ape. 'Let me see you.'

'Why should I? You come closer if you want to see me.' Mowgli pointed at the cubs. 'Let them go! Let them go home and take me!'

'Perhaps,' said the ape. Then he called, loud and sharp: 'Bring him closer to me!'

'Who are you talking to?'

'To them,' said the ape softly. A dozen monkeys suddenly came sliding down the mountainside. Sharp, calloused fingers grabbed at Mowgli and pushed him further towards the cave.

Mowgli swiped at the monkeys furiously. 'Get back! Get back, or I'll set Kaa on you!'

The monkeys spat at him but retreated a few paces.

'He wouldn't!' one hissed.

'He would!' chittered another. 'There isn't nothing a man-cub won't do – we know that by now.'

The darkness of the cave seemed to pulse, and out from its depths there stepped a white shadow.

The ape was twice as tall as Mowgli, and his paws were as large as Mowgli's face. The ape approached on all fours, moving so slowly he seemed more mineral than animal. His back was grey, and his face was white, and his ruby eyes shone out starkly from his face. The hairs on Mowgli's neck stood on end.

'Listen,' said Mowgli. He tried to make his voice sound calm and grown up. 'Give me the cubs. I'll deliver them back to their mother – and then I'll come back!'

'No, no, human child,' said the ape, and his voice creaked with age. 'If I let you go, you will not come back. Do you think I am simple?'

'No! But I—'

'Be silent. Now that you are here, you and the cubs and I will be a family.'

Mowgli reached for his knife at his side. His fingers met only the green harness, wrapped dozens of times around his waist. He whispered something rude in Buffalo. He began to try to untangle it.

'Come closer,' said the ape. 'Let me touch your face.'

'I'm fine here.' Mowgli's blood was racing so fast, he was not sure if his hands and feet would work.

He edged three steps backwards and glanced over the edge of the ledge. He bit his lip again, so hard he tasted blood.

'Don't go so close to the edge!' said the ape querulously. 'Come into the shade! Come and meet your new family.'

Mowgli turned to face the ape head on. 'I already have a family,' he said. 'The jungle is my family.' Then he sprang suddenly across the stone, seized the two cubs, clutched them against his chest and sprinted for the edge of the rock.

'Stop him!' cried the ape. The monkeys let out a screech that shook dust down from the surrounding mountainside and flocked after him.

Mowgli closed his eyes and jumped, throwing his great rope of vines upward as he fell. His back smacked against the great pulsing carpet of birds waiting just below the edge of the rock; they slowed his fall, but he felt himself slipping past them, batting painfully against their beating wings. Then he jerked hard, swinging in the air, the wind jolted out of him.

Fighting for breath, he looked up and saw that three vultures had his coil of rope in their claws. He was dragging them downward, but ever more slowly, and he soon landed on the earth below with a smack that bruised but did not break him.

A shriek of rage and loss came over the cliff edge. 'After them!' called the ape. 'Bandar-log! Bring him back! Bring the man-cub!'

Mowgli jumped to his feet and ducked away from the anxious licking of Baloo and Mother Wolf. He laid down the tiger cubs in the shadow of a tree; they were dazed but alive. 'Stay there,' he said. 'Hide under the leaves and don't squeak.'

He stared up the mountainside. A blur of brown, a mass of arms and legs and tails, was swinging its way down the rock face. It chittered as it came, calling of what they would do when they got hold of Mowgli.

'We'll pull his arms off his back!'

'And chew on his face by the moonlight!'

'They're coming,' said Mowgli. 'The Bandar-log.'

Bagheera looked upward. His eyes were sharper than Mowgli's, and he could see that the onslaught numbered in the hundreds. His hackles rose along his back as he crouched low. He said nothing, only rocked backwards, waiting.

Baloo drew in a breath. 'Do we run? Take the cubs and disappear, and hope the ape and his monkeys will forget?' he asked. 'Or do we fight? And put the fear of the jungle into the vile creatures once and for all?'

He did not really have to ask, but he wanted to hear the spark rise in Mowgli's voice. It filled his old heart with courage.

'Baloo! You no more have to ask the question than I do.' Mowgli looked up at the approaching army. 'The tales all tell the same story: that we fight and keep fighting. Call the jerboas. We'll need them. We're fighting the ape's army.'

Brother Wolf came lolloping up the hill, followed by Father Wolf. 'Are we too late?'

'You are not. The cub has done well.' Raksha's eyes shone out at her family ranged beside her. She moved in front of Mowgli. 'Even so, your skin is no thicker than a newborn rat's, my son, and you have no claws. Stay back.'

Mowgli scoffed. 'I have a knife! And my teeth! And so what if I die? To die in the jungle is a glorious thing!'

Raksha's head jerked round, and she bared her teeth at him. 'Nobody gets to speak with such casual carelessness about the death of my son! Not even my son himself.'

Bagheera padded closer and laid his forehead against Raksha's. His eyes were on the monkeys. 'You know what he means. You taught him yourself, as did I. We are never fighting only for ourselves. We fight for the survivors. Because somebody always survives.'

'Exactly!' Mowgli turned and whispered, grinning, to his wolf brother. 'And actually I very much plan for that somebody to be me.'

And then the monkeys were upon them.

They came like rain from above – rain with claws. Their teeth were sharp and yellow, and their nails were brown. Mowgli was immediately swamped in a pile of seven Bandar-log, each of them chittering and trying to bite his back and neck, to tear off his ears and fingers.

'Call Kaa!' Mowgli panted. 'Tell Kite to call Kaa! The snake will be sleeping – call him anyway!'

Baloo lumbered through the sea of monkeys, slashing with his paws, towards the trees. He set back his great shaggy head and let out the loudest bellow that had been heard in the jungle. 'Bring Kaa!' he called in Kite. 'Bring Kaa!' he called in Jerboa.

Mowgli struggled to his knees, and then to his feet. A monkey darted in and bit with yellow teeth at his ankle. 'Ah!' he cried. The pain of it shot up his leg, and he stumbled. He slashed with his stone knife, and they fell back, but more came – a sea that kept returning to pull and scratch at his naked skin. Mowgli let out a cry of pain as he felt himself lifted from the ground, up towards the cliff.

Bagheera was on the monkeys in a bound. He clamped his jaws around the neck of the largest and flung him from Mowgli's back.

'I will not lose this one too,' he said. 'Get *back*!' And he sent the monkeys flying against the side of the rock.

There was a rustling in the bushes, and a great wave of jerboas and mice and rats came sweeping on to the battleground. They leaped at the monkeys, biting at their paws, causing them to screech in pain and surprise. Some turned and fled into the trees. But still more Bandar-log came, chittering and wailing as they swung down the rock side.

Raksha stayed near the tiger cubs, her hackles on end, swinging at Bandar-log as they came near. 'My child risked his life to rescue these two scraps of orange and black,' she growled. 'Do you think I will give them up to you?'

Mowgli, swiping at a monkey with his knife, spotted sleek skin moving in the trees above them. 'Kaa!' cried Mowgli. 'Over here!'

The great snake came slithering down from the trees, the front half of his vast body already beginning its dance as he reached

the floor. The five monkeys nearest to Kaa froze, wide-eyed, and began to march in ragged lines towards the python's teeth. But the chaos was too much; too many bodies weaved in and out of each other, and the stillness of his dance could not take hold of the horde of Bandar-log.

'Are there more?' gasped Mowgli, his breath ragged. 'Is this all of them, or are there more to come?'

As if in answer, a shrill hoot from the ape came from above. Thirty grey-furred, grey-toothed monkeys – the final reserve – came sweeping over the edge of the cliff towards them.

Bagheera let out a roar so loud it made the ground vibrate under him. He bared his long, fine claws. But his fur was missing in clumps, and his paws shook as he moved in to meet the fresh wave.

'Is there no end?' said Baloo, panting. 'I don't know how much longer we can fight!'

It was true, Mowgli thought. His legs were beginning to quiver with exhaustion under him. He had thought Kaa would be able to save them, but there was too much noise, too much movement

for the snake's charm to work.

The fresh wave of Bandar-log had almost reached the ground. As Mowgli ran at them, he could not suppress a tiny gasp of fear. The monkeys descended, landing on his shoulders and back, and he began to swing wildly with his knife.

It was Raksha who turned the tide of the battle. Before Mother Wolf had been a mother, she was a fighter; now she was both, and there was nothing more deadly in the whole of the jungle.

At the sound of Mowgli's gasp of fear – that slight intake of breath – a great jolt of ferocity shot up into her heart, and she forgot about protecting the tiger cubs, forgot everything in the world except her son.

Raksha gave a howl that was made of love and fury in equal parts and threw herself into the centre of the fray. She was a whirlwind of claws. Her teeth were sharper than those of any wolf in the Pack, and as they slashed and bit at the great sea of monkeys, a terrified cry went up.

'She is possessed!' cried the monkeys. 'The she-wolf is unhinged!'

Raksha leaped over Mowgli's head and landed with her front paws deep in a monkey's chest, her jaws around the neck of a second.

'Up the mountain!' called a second monkey. 'Flee upward!'

'She is a demon!' cried the largest of the grey monkeys. 'Retreat! Retreat!' It retreated, straight into the open jaws of Kaa.

At last there were only a dozen injured monkeys limping wildly for cover.

Baloo's fur was matted, and Bagheera's ear was torn, but they stood tall on either side of Mowgli, staring up at the retreating forces.

Mowgli bent over, speaking through gasps. 'What should we do with the great ape? Do we wait for him to come down the rock to fight? Shall I go up to him?'

'If you will allow me,' said Kaa, '*I* will go to him. I have heard tell of him for many years and have long wished to . . . dance with him.'

Mowgli pressed down on a cut on his chest to stop the bleeding. 'Tell the ape to go back up the mountain and never come back down, and we'll spare his life,' he said to Kaa.

'I could certainly do that,' Kaa acknowledged. And without further words, he began to slide up the rock, his body finding places to grip that were invisible to Mowgli's eyes.

Mowgli turned to Bagheera. 'Is he going to do it?' he asked.

'No,' said Bagheera shortly. 'I would imagine not.' He gave Mowgli one taciturn lick on the back of his arm, to quell a small rivulet of blood, and turned back towards the trees. 'You did not do badly tonight,' he said over his shoulder. 'I am proud, young squirrel.'

The trees around them began to bend as a gentle breeze picked up. Mowgli looked around the battleground, at the stained earth, and the patches of black fur where Baloo and Bagheera had been scraped and torn.

Baloo smiled down at his human student, and then at the host of rodents at his feet. 'I don't know about you,' he said in Jerboa, 'but my mouth-snake is dry, and I wish to be watered. Come, friends. Let's go in search of a drink. Leave the cub with his mother; they need to be alone.'

'Come, Mowgli,' said Raksha. 'We have one last thing to do.

Bring one of the cubs.' She lifted the nearest tiger cub in her mouth, swinging him by the scruff of his neck.

Mowgli scooped the other up in his arms. It was the female cub; she was small enough to sit in his cupped hands, and her fur was soft as water.

It took several hours to find Shere Khan. It was dark when they found him stalking near the river, his tail in the air, sniffing for game.

'Shere Khan!' called Raksha, and she set down the tiger cub.

Mowgli laid the other down, and the cubs sat there, side by side, blinking dazedly at their uncle.

Shere Khan gave a low growl, and the cubs skittered to hide behind Mowgli.

'What do you want?' said the tiger. 'You are not welcome here.'

'Wait until you see what we brought . . .' began Mowgli.

Raksha gently pushed Mowgli aside. Her eyes met the tiger's directly.

'You said, many years ago, that there would be a reckoning,' said Raksha. 'And there have been many. But here is the worst reckoning of all, Shere Khan: a debt.'

'I wouldn't stoop to owe a debt to a wolf,' sneered Shere Khan.

Raksha pushed the tiger cubs forward with her nose. 'These are your kin. Taken by the great white ape you woke. Rescued by the man-cub. Defended by the wolves and the bear and panther and snake.'

Shere Khan said nothing, only rolled back his gums from his teeth. But his eyes, beneath the fury, were stunned.

'The debt will haunt you, Shere Khan,' said Raksha. 'It will itch you at night until you roar to be rid of your own skin. It will follow you through the dark like a snake. It will not die. A debt can be repaid only with generosity, and you have no ounce of that in you.'

Raksha and Shere Khan stared, eye to eye, teeth bared, as they had so many years before.

The tiger looked away first.

And then Raksha turned, with a swish of her ragged grey tail, and prowled back into the jungle, her two-legged son running hard at her side.

❧

It was a dry night that night, and the moon shone so brightly that the whole jungle glowed silver and jade. Mowgli took an armful of leaves and feathers into the crook of a tree and made his bed there. He wanted the night air to soothe his cuts. He piled up a heap of pigeon feathers at one end of the crook and buried his head in it.

The branches rocked lightly under him in time with the wind and the beating heart of the jungle.

Mowgli watched the stars through the gaps in the leaves. They shone so bright a silver that he could see the scrapes on the back of his hand and his pulse beating with such force and joy through his veins.

Someone always survives, he thought. And the stories go on, from one voice to another, up through the jungle canopy and out into the world.